MW01243018

The Quest for Caesar’s Medallion

The Rixey Files Bok One

Hugh Richard Williams

Published by Rogue Phoenix Press. LLP

ISBN: 978-1986908139

Credits
Cover Artist: Designs by Ms G
Editor: Sherry Derr-Wille
Editor: Linda S. Goersch

A Word from the Author

I have written several books in the Zombie Apocalypse genre. In fact, I am still working on the final book of my first series. I hit the wall on that genre but felt like I wanted to keep writing. I have always been a big fan of detective stories, both classic and thriller variations. It seemed like a natural match. Thus, the creation of Miller Rixey occurred. You will see what kind of person he is as you read my story. He has a streak of picaresque in him, as he can be a bit of a rogue when the situation occurs. That having been said, he is a hard-working Private Investigator.

This book would have been impossible without the valuable help of my team of Beta Readers. Grant Elliot Smith gave me incredible insight into the importance of pacing. Bree Pierce, Kathy Dinisi, Stephen W. Smith, Pam Bingle Finch, Mary Brueckner, Elizabeth Holman Collins, Christopher Manny, Shirley Nanos, Sarah Moskowitz Hocking, and Elizabeth Stewart also provided me very valuable ideas and pointers. Geoffrey S. Jade Barrett has given me tremendous insight into the publishing business and supported me the whole way. Also, thanks to the many friends, too numerous to mention, who I discussed the book with and gave me great ideas about situations.

Finally, though my books are in fiction genres, I do my best to make them believable. This is achieved by doing research on the various locations my characters visit as well as the items that they use. Sit back now and enjoy.

S/ Hugh Richard Williams 2/13/17 Carbondale, Illinois

Chapter One

"Every new beginning comes from some other beginning's end." Seneca

"Miller Rixcy?" The ICU nurse called my name.

"Yes." I put down my newspaper and rushed to the counter, anticipating the worst.

"You may see Mr. Bishop now," she said with a smile.

"Is he okay? Is he going to make it?"

The nurse's smile quickly left her face. The bullet has been removed and is still in critical condition... but he is awake."

I rushed through the doors and was escorted to the ICU room. I saw him there, hooked up to all the wires, my heart sunk. The beeping from his various machines did not help my mood any. His eyes were closed and his face was bruised and swollen. I walked to his bedside. "Willard?"

The nurse said, "He may not be very coherent at this point."

Willard opened his eyes and focused on my face. "Hey kid, good to see you." He groaned and sat up in his bed. He looked a little unsteady but in his condition; who wouldn't look that way?

"Glad you are still with us," I said, choking back my emotions. Willard Bishop had been my friend, my boss, and my mentor for the past sixteen years. I always thought he was invincible. He was one of the best Private Investigators that I had ever known and he had taught me so much.

"You cannot get rid of me that easy, kid, "Bishop said in a raspy voice and then began coughing. The commotion brought a couple of ICU nurses into the room. "Kid, come here...," Bishop said, struggling with the ICU nurses attempts to lay him down. "I'm fine, leave me alone," he rasped.

I went up to his bed as he held out his hand. He dropped a set of keys into along with a piece of paper into my hand. "The Agency's yours now. I'm getting too old for this shit."

I started to say something to him, but I thought better of it and remained silent. No one ever won an argument with Willard Bishop. I took the keys and nodded as the nurses pushed me out of the room. At the door, there were other nurses and a doctor rushing to enter.

I held the keys and the piece of paper in my hand and walked back to the waiting area. I flopped down on a couch. My head was spinning. I knew I had to collect myself. I was soon lost in my thoughts. Memories of my first meeting with Bishop came to mind. Sixteen years ago, I was attending Illinois State University where I majored in Criminal Justice. I had always been a big fan of detective stories and had no desire to teach, become a cop or a correctional officer. My degree in Criminal Justice would mean that I would only have to apprentice for one year instead of the usual three years to get my license. I began sending resumes and cover letters to well over one hundred detective agencies. I thought I would get lots of offers since after all, I had excellent grades and strong recommendations. I was wrong. I got one offer. It was from The Bishop Agency. It was an offer for a paid summer internship worth $5000 if I passed the interview and he decided to hire me. My initial excitement at the meeting faded when I saw the Agency was located in Carbondale, Illinois. It was hardly the bustling metropolis I had envisioned working in when I sent out my resumes. I thought to myself, well you aren't exactly flush with offers, why not check it out?

I made the decision to interview for the job and that moment changed my life forever. I wasn't sure what to expect when I arrived in Carbondale, Illinois. I wondered what working in a small town like Carbondale could offer me. I knew from the letter; the Agency was located in a section in the city the locals called "The Strip." I walked up and down the strip finally locating a non-descript building that had "The Bishop Agency" proudly emblazoned on the door. I had been to Carbondale plenty of times before to visit friends. I guess I had even walked past the building quite a few times and never noticed it. I later found out this was not by accident; it was by design. I pushed the door open and walked in. I shivered as I felt the cold blast from the air conditioning. I heard a bell tinkle.

The reception area seemed rather bleak. A manual typewriter rested on a cheap fabricated wood desk. There was also what looked like a very old and battered landline also seated on the desk. I saw five old file cabinets that looked like they had seen better days. Five folding chairs completed what I would call the "Early Depression" look. I noticed four what appeared to be office doors behind the desk. I wondered to myself if I had made a mistake even coming down to Carbondale since it had been about a four-hour drive for me.

A beautiful red headed woman was sitting at the front desk. Her nameplate read "Ms. Nickels." She appeared to be a forty-something in terms of her age. She looked up and smiled briefly at me. I doffed my fedora as I introduced myself and showed her the letter I had received from Mr. Bishop. She nodded as she quickly read the letter and then she pointed to a door that said "Mr. Bishop Private" and told me to go in and that I was expected. Out of habit, I knocked and when I heard "Come," came the booming voice from behind the door. I entered.

In the large, well-lighted office, a man in his fifties sat behind a wooden desk. He motioned me to a seat as he was talking on the phone. I looked for a place to put my fedora and saw a hat rack. I flipped it toward the hat rack and to my pleasure and surprise, it landed right where I had tossed it. I sat in the chair in front of the desk that was unexpectedly comfortable. I looked around the room to pass the time as I waited for Mr. Bishop to get finished with his phone call. Maybe the way his office was set up would give me some insight into the man I was about to interview? I hoped so.

Bishop's office was in sharp contrast to the reception area. It was well lit. He had two laptops sitting on his desk as well as what looked like two monitors. There was also what looked like a state-of-the-art desktop on a smaller desk behind him. The office was undoubtedly lavishly furnished. The forestry class I had taken during my Freshman year in college told me the desk was made of teak or some other precious hardwood. The walls were lined with cedar. I looked around the walls of the office and saw three oil paintings. It looked like Bishop had a rather eclectic taste in art. Where these really a Pollock, a Picasso, and a Warhol I was seeing hanging on the walls? I thought, perhaps a better time for that question later. I saw three pieces of sculpture that I could not immediately place, but they did look familiar.

I quickly turned my attention to his desk. I saw what I knew to be an expensive humidor. I saw three signed baseballs from Ty Cobb, Honus Wagner, and Babe Ruth. They all resided in plastic cubes with their certificates of authenticity being prominently displayed. I also saw a pen holder on the desk and as I love using fountain pens immediately recognized two Mont Blanc's, a very nice Cross fountain pen and a Waterman fountain pen. I wasn't sure what to make of what I had seen, but my interest had been piqued. There was no doubt that Mr. Bishop was a fascinating man.

Bishop finished with his call and cleared his throat to let me know the interview had begun. He opened a drawer and pulled out a file that was a couple of inches thick. I saw my name on it. I hadn't realized I had been alive long enough to have merited a file that size. Did I wonder what type of person would have the resources and contacts to build a file that size on me? I shrugged, well I was here, let's see what happens.

"Miller, may I call you Miller?" Bishop began.

"Yes, Mr. Bishop." I looked him over and decided I was having a hard time placing this guy. He could have been anywhere from forty to sixty. He had a full head of gray hair and it looked like three days' growth. He seemed to be in pretty good shape.

He smiled at me and picked up a pair of reading glasses. He opened the file and began, "Before we get too far along, I wish to give you an option." I saw him slide a check toward me. It was made out to me in the amount of five thousand dollars. "If you choose to, you may take this check and head back to Normal and there will be no hard feelings. Believe me, I know being a private detective isn't for everyone."

I frowned and said slowly, "Well, your offer is generous to be sure. Don't get me wrong, it would be great to have five thousand in my pocket and to be able to goof off this summer, but I decided I wanted to be a private detective, yours was the only firm that even sent me a positive reply. You must have seen something in me the other agencies didn't. Let's continue with the interview and see where it leads." I shifted uneasily in my chair and looked Mr. Bishop in the eye. "How does that sound to you?" I asked.

Mr. Bishop broke out in a smile, "Excellent. I like your attitude, young man. You can call me Willard."

"Thank you, Willard."

" I see you have excellent grades in college, but shall we say your grades and ACT score in high school left something to be desired. Care to elaborate on this?" Willard asked.

I looked back at Willard, "I hated high school and did not take enough classes to do well on my ACT. The school counselor told my parents and that I was bored and did not feel challenged. I shrugged, "She could have been right. Anyway, my parents are both alums from Illinois State and pulled some strings and got me in." I laughed, "I'm sure you had all of this in your file."

"Yes. You are quite right, but I put a huge premium on talking to people. You know what I mean, gives me a better feel for them rather than simply reading about their records in black and white."

I nodded and adjusted my position in the chair as I awaited his next question.

He thumbed through my file and making a sort of a raspy laugh, continued, "I see you have a Carry Conceal Permit. That's a good start. It shows me you know a little something about basic weapon safety. What is your weapon of choice?" he asked.

I carry a Ruger LCR .38 special."

"Somehow, I would have been surprised if you carried a semi-automatic. It wouldn't fit your personality," Willard replied.

I looked at him, somewhat confused.

He pointed to my fedora on the rack and the fountain pens in my pocket, "You seem like kind of a retro guy. I have the feeling you would have been more at home in the 50's."

Willard thumbed through my file, "You seem like a good kid. Your teachers speak highly of you. You sure you wouldn't be happier in law school or perhaps working on a Ph.D.? I can probably get you into any school you would want. Teaching and the law are honorable professions."

I winced at the "kid" remark. I wondered who this guy was who said he could get me into any school I wanted. "Thanks, I really appreciate your offer, but I want to give being a private detective a try. It may not turn out to be what I wanted, but trying it is the only way I will ever find out," I replied.

Willard stood up and walked over to where I had been sitting. He reached into his desk and pulled out a bundle of paperwork. "Please fill out these forms before you leave. They are pretty standard. The most important is the confidentiality agreement. I'm guessing you want to get college credit for your work this summer. Fill out the enrollment form for Illinois State and submit that form along with the letter Ms. Nickels has waiting for you when you leave my office. You will be getting four hours' credit for your internship. That should about cover everything." He stood up and shook my hand. "Welcome to The Bishop Agency. We will see you back in two weeks. Do you have any questions?" he asked with a broad smile on his face.

"None that I can think of."

Willard concluded, "You are certainly free to tell your friends and your parents that my agency has agreed to hire you for the summer. The only thing I ask is that you refrain from discussing with them about what you have seen in my office and your theories of what is going on here. Fair enough? I try not to impose too many restrictions on young interns such as yourself. I find that it sometimes inhibits them, which gives me a harder time trying to evaluate them."

I laughed, "Fair enough Willard. I don't know enough to form any type of theories as to what is going on here. All I know is this is a detective agency and that you hired me to work for you as an intern for the summer."

"Good boy," he beamed.

I felt a gentle nudge that broke me out of my reverie. I looked around wildly to get my bearings. I was still at the hospital. That had been one interesting dream.

A concerned looking, motherly type nurse looked down at me. "Young man, there is nothing you can do for your friend here. I can appreciate your concerns. Don't worry, we have the best doctors looking out for him. Go home and get some rest, we will keep you informed."

I nodded and thanked her. She was right, there was nothing I could do for Bishop here. I decided my time would be better spent at the office. Since Willard had now put me in charge of it, I was sure I had a lot of catching up to do. Being in the office and reviewing Willard's files might give me some insight into why he had been attacked. While maybe the local police were all too anxious to write the attack off as a simple mugging, I had my doubts. I got up and rode the elevator down to the ground floor. I barely noticed the hum of the electric door as they swung open as I left the hospital. I spotted by SUV in the parking lot and headed toward it.

Chapter Two

"If a man says a thing often enough, he is very likely to acquire some sort of faith in it sooner or later." Dashiell Hammett

I got into my SUV and started the engine. I took my time heading back to now was my agency. I arrived in time to see two men dressed like painters leaving the office. I parked in back and saw Ms. Nickels sitting at her desk in the reception area rather than her office. I heard a click of the door and when I pushed it open, I heard the familiar tinkle of a bell. It was apparent Ms. Nickels had been crying. Her eyes looked red and bloodshot. She reached for a tissue and forced a smile.

I tried to give her a reassuring smile.

"Is he going to be alright," she sniffled. It was easy to see she had been crying. "I had gotten word that the surgery had at least removed the bullet." The phone rang, but Ms. Nickels let it ring through and it eventually went to voicemail. This was not like her at all.

"A little worse for the wear. I talked to him and he seemed lucid. I'm sure he will be fine; he has the constitution of a horse," I said in my most reassuring voice.

"I hope you are right." She dabbed her eyes and then proceeded to continue her work.

I headed to my office and stood there confused when I saw my name had been taken off the door. Ms. Nickels softly laughed as she sensed my confusion.

"Mr. Rixey, there is your new office," Ms. Nickels said pointing at the door that had been Willard's office. I now had an explanation for why the painters had been there. The door now read: Mr. Rixey and right below my name was the word Private.

I turned to Ms. Nickels, "It's Miller all these years, and now Mr. Rixey?"

"Yes, sir. Mr. Bishop called and told me about his plans. You are the boss now, so it becomes Mr. Rixey. I took the liberty of having your personal items moved to into your new office. Mr. Bishop 's things are still in there. Is that going to be a problem?"

I shook my head no. "Not in the least. I have some things to work out, so please no calls unless it's crucial." With that, I pushed my office open and took my seat behind the desk. I fished the piece of paper that Willard had forced on me. It quite simply said, Kaplan Cleaning Company a phone number and what looked to be a code word. I committed the number to memory and burned the paper in an ashtray.

My mind was so exhausted that it was a struggle for me to think. I punched up Willard's caseload and found no active cases listed for the past few weeks. I frowned to myself, I thought he told me he had been working on a divorce case. I checked his visitor's log and saw one name in the past few weeks, Robert Layne. I knew Willard had been a stickler for keeping accurate records, well at least when it came to caseloads and client lists. As I pondered what I hadn't found, I put my legs up on the desk in an attempt to relax.

The next thing I remembered hearing was the buzzer in my office. I almost fell out of my chair to answer it. "Yes, Ms. Nickels, I take it's something important, if not otherwise please handle it yourself. I am going to be busy the next few hours orienting myself. I trust your judgment."

"A Mr. Layne is here to see Mr. Bishop, I thought it would be best for you to explain to him the current situation." Luckily for me, neither she nor Mr. Layne could see the grimace I made. I was already under the gun.

"Quite right. Please send Mr. Layne in." I really wasn't in the mood to meet with anyone today, but now it was my Agency and I had obligations. Who knows, maybe Mr. Layne is somehow involved in what happened to Willard?

I got to my feet and made an attempt to make myself look somewhat presentable. My hair was a mess, I had not shaved in a week, and I was wearing the same clothes that I had on yesterday. Not exactly the impression you want to make with a new client. I had a feeling Mr. Layne was one of Willard's special clients. I did not want to make a bad impression for either Willard's sake or the Agency's sake, or least of all for my sake. Think positive thoughts, I told myself.

I heard a firm knock on my door.

I checked myself one more time in an office mirror and then said, "Come."

Chapter Three

"The world is full of obvious things which nobody by any chance ever observes. Arthur Conan Doyle, The Hound of the Baskervilles

A distinguished looking gentleman of about fifty years entered my office. He was about 6'2, medium build, clean shaven and had a head full of gray hair. The man reeked money and influence. This is a good sign for any private detective. I knew he would not be quibbling with me over an extra night in a hotel room as part of my expenses as some of my other less fortunate clients had.

I held out my hand, "Miller Rixey, and you would be?"

"None of your business. I am here to talk to Mr. Bishop. I do not talk to the help. Get Mr. Bishop here right now," he roared.

I frowned, "Mr. Bishop is lying in a hospital bed recovering from a gunshot wound and a severe beating. He is currently unavailable. I am now in charge of this Agency and I saw that you had visited Mr. Bishop about a week ago, if you wish to do business with us, you will have to deal with me, "I spoke assertively.

The man became apologetic. It became apparent he wasn't used to people talking to him the way I had.

He extended his hand. I am Mr. Layne. I am very sorry to hear about Willard. Please send him my best wishes."

I took his hand and shook. "Nice to meet you, sir. I assure you that I will pass those on to Mr. Bishop."

Mr. Layne asked, his eyes darted back and forth to the sides of this office, "Is this room secure?"

I nodded, "I sweep it every day." I pointed to the humidor. "That doubles as a white noise generator. I also have electronic protection on every window in the office. I just have one more thing I do. I know Mr. Bishop didn't do it." I reached into my desk and found my electronic wand. I was grateful that Ms. Nickels had seen to it to move my items to my new office. "Please remain standing. I turned the wand on and ran it over him. When I came to a large stickpin on his jacket, the rod went bonkers.

"What is that, "I asked pointing to the stickpin.

"Oh, it's an old family heirloom. It has our coat of arms on it as you can tell."

"Okay, not a problem." I made a gesture to him to remove the stick pin and hand it to me. I silently placed it in a bag designed for the purpose and then put the bag in a canister. I would return it to him later with a caution. I still didn't want the whoever was listening to realize what I had discovered. Let them think it was a temporary mechanical error.

"I am guessing it's safe to say that you wore that same pin when you met with Mr. Willard?"

"Umm. Yes. I wear it wherever I go. Why is that a problem?" He looked confused.

"Yes. It's a bigtime problem. According to the readout I got on the wand, electrical pulses were emitting from it. In other words, you had a bigger audience than FOX. Someone substituted pins on you I am afraid. So, whoever was listening in heard everything you said to Mr. Bishop, word for word.

I was shocked when the man actually broke into a smile, "Thank you for making that discovery. This is most embarrassing. I assume I have your complete discretion on this matter?"

I nodded, "The Bishop Agency is the soul of discretion."

"Excellent, I see the things I have heard about your competence are all true." He took my hand and shook it. "My name is Robert Layne. But call me Bobby. I have an assignment that someone with your talents may be the only person who can help me."

"Thank you, Bobby, please have a seat. It's a pleasure to meet you. Can I get you anything? Coffee, Water, Tea, or perhaps a Monte Cristo, from the Dominican Republic, with Cuban seeds?" I asked doing my bit to be the gracious host. Customer service was always number one at The Bishop Agency.

He shook his head as he nervously looked at his watch. After we were both seated, I asked him to begin. I took out a notepad and a pen and waited.

"Your mentor was Willard Bishop, correct?" Bobby asked in a cracked voice.

I nodded, "Is, I corrected. I have worked with him for the past sixteen years."

"So, you have been handling highly classified matters for some time, I take it? He stammered, "I mean, umm well you..."

I nodded. I could see he was very nervous and now did my best to put him at ease.

"Bobby, I am guessing you are a scotch drinker? I asked as I pushed a buzzer on my desk, "Ms. Nickels, when you get a moment, would you please bring in a couple of glasses and a bottle of Macallan."

Bobby nodded.

"This will help you relax some and then we can get on to the reason you made this trip to rural Carbondale. I laughed attempting to relax the mood in the office, "I see you as more of a big city type of person. More of a New York, LA, or a Chicago type of person, correct?"

He nodded. A few minutes later there was a knock on the door. "Come," I said. Ms. Nickels wordlessly came in with a tray with two glasses and a bottle of 18-year-old Macallan on it. She sat the tray down on my desk, smiled at me, and then left. I poured a drink for me and one for Bobby and sat back.

"Perhaps a short respite is in order. Nothing like a good drink to settle the nerves," I said.

I wondered what could possibly cause a man who is obviously so powerful to be so nervous and to get him to pay me a visit in Carbondale.

I took out a cigar from the humidor and squeezed it. Still fresh. I cut off the end using my cigar cutters. I ran my lighter over the bottom of the cigar. This guaranteed a smooth smoke. I lit the front end and plopped it in my mouth. I took a few puffs waiting for Bobby to compose himself.

Bobby reached for a glass and quickly gulped it down. I picked up my glass and began slowly drinking it. "Feeling better, I hope?" I asked Bobby. "I know an occasional drink of fine liquor can smooth over hard to discuss areas."

Somewhat red-faced, he said in a shaky voice, "Yes, I am, thank you."

"Well then, let's continue. I need to know everything you told Mr. Bishop," I said with a smile.

"What do you know about ancient Rome?"

"I shrugged, "Mainly what I learned in my Western Civilization class when I was in college. Founded about 753 BC by two legendary brothers, Romulus and Remus. The Romans were at one point the most powerful empire in the history of the world. Their empire finally fell in 476 AD. There was an Eastern Empire that ended sometime in the 1450s. That 's about it."

"Very good. You've heard of Julius Caesar?"

I smiled, "I have always been a history buff, so yes. The Gallic Wars, the Ides of March, and so on...," my voice trailed off.

Bobby nodded. "You would be surprised at how many people of your generation haven't, or maybe you wouldn't. He leaned forward in his chair and began.

"This is where our story begins. During the Gallic Wars, there was a Legatus legioni's named Aetius Caecus." He was the head of a legion, what in English we would call a Legate. He reportedly saved Caesar 's life while the battle seemed to be going badly for the Romans. Caesar rewarded Caecus with a large land grant in what we now call France."

I leaned forward, picked up the scotch bottle and poured him another glass.

Bobby nodded, picked up the glass and continued," Caecus soon became a very wealthy man and decided to show his mentor how he felt about him by giving him a wonderful medal. The Medallion was in the shape of a circle with a circumference of about six inches. It was made of solid gold. It weighed about eight ounces. The front side was a picture of Caesar wearing a wreath on his head. The wreath was made of diamonds. The obverse of the Medallion was covered in emeralds, rubies, and sapphires around the edges. The reverse had an inscription in Latin:

"*Magistro meo et amico Julius Caesar*" which in English: "To my mentor and friend, Julius Caesar." There was a second line on the reverse: "*EGO eram laetus ut servo vos quod gratias ago vos pro vestri remuneror oh valde Caesar.* In English," I was glad to serve you and thank you for your reward, oh great Caesar." It is attached to a gold chain about eight inches. The chain is made of eighteen karat gold. Legend has it that Caesar was very proud of the gift and wore in all the time. It became known as Caesar 's Medallion. He was even supposed to have been wearing it when he was stabbed to death on the Ides of March. When his body was found, the Medallion had vanished."

"That's a fascinating story, Bobby. What does it have to do with Mr. Bishop or me, for that matter?"

"Let me finish my tale and my need for your services will become clearer to you."

Bobby leaned closer to me as he spoke, now somewhat excitedly, "As I said earlier, when Caesar died, the Medallion was nowhere to be found. While there had been rumors as to its location, no one could be sure if the item even existed or if it was merely a legend. The Medallion finally shows up at an auction at Sotheby's auction house in 1775. That is where the formal provenance begins. It's sold to a Lord Hiram James. The auction price, according to the records, was 75 pounds' sterling. In today's money that would be about USD 165,000. Hardly an insignificant amount considering the timeframe of the sale. According to legends, the Medallion seemed to have been cursed. Supposedly, any who owned the Medallion died a very violent death. No one knows if the legends are true, but what happened to the four most recent owners seems to give the story some credence. Anyway, James was murdered about six months later. The James family fearing there was some sort of curse behind the Medallion, quickly sold it to another English Lord. The purchaser died in a very suspicious accident about a year later. Caesar's Medallion did not surface again until 1819 where it was sold again at auction to a private buyer for an undisclosed price. Nothing more of it was heard of for 103 years. From what my researchers found out; the owner had been another English nobleman who had the bad luck of being stampeded to death by a herd of his bulls. We cannot be positive about what happened to the Medallion, but it dropped out of sight.

In 1922, the Medallion reappeared and was sold by private treaty in Istanbul to an American named Randall Jackson. In 1937, Jackson was found murdered in his mansion. The initial report treated his death as being involved in a home invasion or burglary that had gone terribly wrong.

When the house and property of Jackson were searched, nothing of value except for the Medallion seemed to be missing. Jackson had art collection insured for $20,000,000 and a coin collection insured for $10,000,00. Both were left untouched. He had kept the Medallion in a special security case. The Medallion had been insured for $2,000,000 by Lloyds of London. Its value was derived from its history. They p aid off the claim in 1938. The fact that neither collection had not been touched seemed to have given credibility to the argument that the and only the Medallion was the target of the robbery. Mr. Jackson took extraordinary care to protect the Medallion as he was familiar with the history of it. He kept it in a special bulletproof, bombproof case. The lock was supposedly impossible to pick.

The rumor was it had been taken by a special squad of Nazis who searched the world for mystical artifacts. What we do know is this, Heinrich Himmler presented the Medallion to Adolph Hitler for this birthday in 1937. I saw captured Nazi film footage of the presentation. My researchers broke down the film. They took still pictures of every frame. There is no doubt that Himmler presented Caesar's Medallion to Hitler at that ceremony."

"Very impressive research, indeed. Please continue."

"Caesar's Medallion has not been seen since 1945. When the Russians finally entered Hitler's bunker, there was no trace of the Medallion. It was known to those in his inner circle that the Medallion was his favorite item. The absence of the Medallion is often used in the argument that both Hitler and Eva, along with top Nazis like Martin Bormann, Eichmann, and Mengele, escaped to South Amer ica." Bobby sat back in his chair, his story told. He reached for the scotch bottle and poured himself another drink.

I squinted and Bobby, "A little late in the game to be hunting down Adolf Hitler and the rest." I paused," I am guessing you want me to find Caesar's Medallion and return it to you?"

Bobby nodded, "Yes. I need to return it to our government so it can be studied."

"Our government being the United States of America, I hope?" I asked.

"Yes," Bobby replied somewhat taken aback.

"What's there to study? I mean it's just some metal and jewels, right, Bobby?" I mean, we all know that it's a rare artifact, right?" I asked. I could feel the temperature drop twenty degrees in the room. There was something he wasn't telling me. It wouldn't be the first time a client either lied to me or forgot to tell me the whole truth. It came with the job.

Bobby chuckled, "That's way beyond my pay grade. What I will tell you is this. The estimated value of the Medallion is $30,000,000. The value comes its historic status. The metal and the jewels are in the neighborhood of $150,000. We are prepared to advance you $100,000 as a nonrefundable retainer as well as $50,000 to cover expenses. If you recover Caesar's Medallion, another 3,000,000 will be paid to you. I believe ten percent is a standard recovery number in your line of work, isn't it?" Bobby asked.

I nodded. "I'll be working for the U.S. government, right?"

Bobby nodded, "Well, as a contractor, yes. You will have no official status, naturally."

Then I will need the following I insisted, "First, I need a diplomatic passport just in case I get jammed up overseas. I have a feeling I will be doing some traveling. Second, I will need someone to be able to hand me a gun when I land where I am going. Unless you are doing something special for me, I will not be able to get a gun aboard my flight. Finally, I will need a contact who is reliable and able to take care of themselves. I don't know anyone I would trust for an assignment like this and this isn't going to be a one-person show."

"The passport will not be a problem. As you will be flying commercial, we will have someone waiting for you with a gun. I imagine it will be what you currently carry? Then you will have no more concerns about your requirements?" I do not want anything to go wrong on this assignment," Mr. Layne stated firmly.

"No. That will be fine. Nothing will go wrong. You will find that I am a most competent operative, "I tersely replied.

"Your first stop will be in Buenos Aires. We will have your contact waiting for you at the airport. She will be looking for you." He reached into his shirt pocket and pulled out a picture and handed it to me. "Her name is Morgan Burke. She should meet all of your needs. She is an experienced problem solver."

"She will know how to get us to Mar Del Plata?"

Bobby looked surprised, "What made you say that?"

"That's where Hitler made a short and initial stop when he arrived in Argentina after he escaped from Berlin at the end of WWII. I am a firm believer in starting at the beginning. I was already pretty sure Hitler didn't die in his bunker and your comments about how much he treasured Caesar's Medallion makes my beliefs even stronger. I do love my conspiracy theories, especially when they turn out to be true. I have done a lot of reading on the topic and Mar Del Plata is where his trail begins."

I reached for the intercom on my desk, "Ms. Nickels, please hold all calls."

"Yes, sir."

"You are a wealth of knowledge, Mr. Rixey. I am glad we will be working together." He reached into his side pocket and pulled out a leather passport holder. "Go ahead and open it," Bobby said.

I did as he told and saw the brown cover of a diplomatic passport. I opened it up and it had Willard's picture and correct information on it. I nodded, "I will need one with my picture and information on it. I also saw first class tickets for Buenos Aires. "One stop flight to Buenos Aires, leaving at 5:30 AM my time from Saint Louis in three days." I could see that someone had some connections. "This looks like a top-flight operation," I wanly smiled. "I assume my tickets will reflect the same schedule that was on these tickets with my name on them instead of his?"

Bobby nodded, "That is the least of our problems. Is there anything else I can do to expedite your mission?" We are most anxious to recover this artifact.

One more thing I cautioned, "Someone or some group had an interest in the recovery of the Medallion. Say nothing about what you have learned about your stickpin. I will give it back to you at the end of our conversation and the whoever is listening will simply think there was a malfunction that occurred."

Three more things, Mr. Rixey, "First, Ms. Burke will be meeting you at the airport. Second, she has been fully briefed. Finally, we will have your passport and tickets delivered by courier by this time tomorrow. As for your retainer and expense money, that too will be delivered in cash at the same time. That's your preferred mode of payment, correct?"

"Yes, it is," I smiled. "Cash has a way of making things less complicated if you follow me."

Bobby nodded," I assume if you aren't here, Ms. Nickels can sign? I know she has worked for your firm for quite some time." Without bothering to wait for an answer, he continued. "It's not my habit to wish anyone luck, so I won't begin today. You seem very competent and I am sure you will do a good job for us."

Our conversation finished, I handed Bobby back his pin. We shook hands and I watched him put the pin back in his lapel as he turned around and walked out of my office.

I knew where Willard had kept his safe. I sat down on the floor, cross-legged, and worked the key into the lock. The door swung open. It made sense to me if he had taken the job, he would have already had his research done. The top level of the safe was crammed with cash. The second level had some very expensive watches and rings. I found what I was looking for on the third level. I saw two folders. One was a couple of inches thick and one was about an inch thick. I pulled them both out. Then following office protocol, I relocked the safe and spun the tumblers. The first one said, Burke, Morgan. The second one said, Hitler in Argentina, 1945-1964. I gasped when I saw the title of the second file. I gathered the two files up, stood, and went to my desk and took a seat.

I didn't realize that once I opened the Hitler file, my life would never be the same again. I really had no choice but to read it. Willard had gone to great pains to secure this file and he did everything for a reason.

Chapter Four

"New Roads; new ruts." G.K. Chesterton

"Ms. Nickels, do you have anything important or pending right now?"

No sir. I am up to date on all my work."

"Very good. Ms. Nickels, please bring me in a pot of coffee along with cream and sugar. I have some important reading to do. Once you have done that, take the rest of the day off. I am sure Willard, I mean Mr. Bishop, would love to see you."

"Are you sure, Mr. Rixey?"

"Yes, quite sure, Ms. Nickels. You have been working much too hard as of late. As I am the boss, consider it an order," I added with a chuckle.

I sat at my desk trying to piece everything I thought I knew. First, Willard was not working on any divorce case. That was simply a ruse to protect Ms. Nickels and me from whoever wanted to stop him on his real mission on the theory that if we didn't know anything, whoever attacked him would leave the agency and us alone. This behavior did not seem like the Willard I had gotten to know over the years. He had always been very forthright as to take me into his confidence about all his cases. What made this case different?

Second, as Bobby, due to his carelessness, had allowed his entire interview to be broadcast, someone with a vested interest in seeing that the Medallion was not recovered knew exactly what Willard and Layne had planned to do.

Third, this is a problem. Willard has a reputation as being one of the finest Private Investigators in the world. If word got out on what Willard had been working on when he was either murdered or shot and beaten up, only a total dumbass, someone like me would take the case. The smarter ones would know better.

Finally, whoever attacked Willard, assuming my theory about why he was attacked was correct, didn't know him very well. They were unable to find his office keys and his safe key. If they had been able to recover the keys, neither of these files would have still been in the safe, not to mention the cash. Well, my theory made sense to me for what it was worth. I knew I would have to pay Willard at least one more visit before I left.

Lies have their places and at times can be very valuable. A disguise is a form of a lie and telling someone a blatant falsehood to protect you or a client are examples of useful lies. When you are analyzing a situation, it's crucial never lie to yourself. You have to study the matter in a detached manner. Lying to yourself will only succeed in giving you a lousy analysis and that will get you killed on a mission as dangerous as this one appeared to be.

I had just reached into my humidor and selected a cigar when I heard a knock on the door.

"Come."

Ms. Nickels entered the room complete with a tray with the pot of coffee I had asked for as well as the cream and sugar. She set the tray on my desk. "Anything else Mr. Rixey?"

"Just lock up, set the security alarms and enjoy the rest of the day as best you can." I pointed to the two files on my desk, "These will keep me very busy.

"Thank you, Mr. Rixey."

I watched her walk out of the office and heard her close the door behind her. A few minutes later, I heard her setting the alarm on the door and the door closing behind her.

I poured a cup of coffee and fixed it the way I liked it and decided to read the file, Hitler in Argentina 1945-1964 first.

I flipped to the first page and saw a very primitive looking Top-

Secret coversheet. It had a description of what the item was, in this case, a letter. The number of copies, which was two, the date the document had been created, September 1, 1945, and a description of the topic of the document: HITLER ESTABLISHED BASECAMP. There was a to and from that were very troubling names: Harry S. Truman was the receiver of this report and J. Edgar Hoover was the sender. Under the checked out to list I saw two signatures that didn't ease my mind, Allen Dulles and John Dulles. Allen Dulles had been the head of Swiss Operations for the OSS during World War II. His job involved gathering intelligence on the Germans and as such had developed a cozy relationship between himself and several high-level Nazis such as Martin Bormann. He later became the first civilian Director of the CIA, serving from 1953-1961. His brother, John Dulles had served as Secretary of State under President Eisenhower. These two were definitely players in the American intelligence field.

Both men held Anti-Semitic views and were suspected of being pro-Nazi. The men saw Nazism as a better alternative to Russian Communism. Pre-WW II saw the explosion of German sympathizer groups like the German-American Bund. This thinking was not merely restricted to the common man. Such American luminaries like Joseph Kennedy, the father of a future President, Charles Lindbergh, and Walt Disney all held similar views. I remembered back to one of my history classes. My professor said had it not been for Pearl Harbor, Germany might have easily won World War II. I suspected she was right.

The report had not been declassified, I double checked for that. I wondered how Willard had managed to get me a copy of it? I knew that Willard had friends who worked in the intelligence field. It was something I would have to ask him about the next time I saw him. The letter, more of a memo actually was short and to the point:

"Mr. President:

This is to inform you that Adolph Hitler has been safely ensconced in the Eden Hotel. It is located in the town of La Falda which is approximately 450 miles from Buenos Aires. He is secure there as the hotel is own by the Einhorn family. Herr Hitler has been very helpful with our plan to gather up the top scientists, their research, and whatever advanced weaponry. This program is being carried out under the auspices of

Operation Paperclip. For the time being, the fact that Hitler committed suicide in Berlin continues to be accepted by the world and offers his best chance for safety.

Further updates will be provided in person by me. This is much too sensitive of a matter for any more communications in writing. If you have any further questions concerning this matter, please contact me and we will discuss any future developments in person. You will be informed in writing of any other new events. Only you and your successors will be cleared to have knowledge about this operation. Allen and John are coordinating the project overseas and I am handling the project in America. I realize that you may have some concerns on Operation Paperclip, but its continuation will help America defeat the Red Menace.

S/ J. Edgar Hoover."

There was a second letter. It was dated October 1, 1945. It too was labeled Top Secret. It had been addressed to President Truman again and had been sent to him by Allen Dulles with a notification that a copy had been sent to J. Edgar Hoover. This one briefly outlined the escape of Hitler from Germany. The title for this was HITLER'S ESCAPE DETAILS FROM BORMANN DIARY.

"President Truman:

As to how Hitler and his entourage escaped Germany, they were able to escape their bunker to a private airport that had not yet fallen under Russian control. The billions of dollars in money, precious metals, gems, and artwork that had been appropriated by Germany had been sent off to Argentina weeks earlier when it became apparent to Martin Bormann that the war was lost. I had arranged for a false weather report to be sent to Allied intelligence which created a situation that grounded their flights. This allowed the three planes that carried Hitler and his entourage to fly to Spain quickly. Once they arrived in Spain, they used two U-Boats for the rest of the journey. This report has been taken directly from Martin Bormann. Please note, we have been greatly helped by both Juan and Evita Peron. Without their help, we would have never been able to place Hitler in Argentina. We need to do our best to keep them if not in power, close to the power. Please let me know if you have any other questions. I will be able to arrange a meeting at your convenience.

S/Allen Dulles."

There was one final letter that was dated 15 December 1964. It had been addressed to Lyndon Johnson and had been sent from John A. McCone who was the director of the CIA. It was also acknowledged that Allen Dulles and J. Edgar Hoover had read the letter. It was entitled: HILTER EVACUATION.

"Hitler was had to be moved to a Bavarian-styled mansion at Inalco, a remote and barely accessible spot at the northwest end of Lake Nahuel Huapi, close to the Chilean border. It was the only facility we could find that would offer much better security and had room enough for his labs and a large number of his entourage and scientists. We are confident that this area is indeed secure and don't envision any more security problems from this location. Security was broken by a captured Nazi war criminal who confessed Hitler's location to the Mossad.

S/ John A. McCone."

If this is really true, I thought, I could see why no one would want this out.

The rest of the file consisted of non-classified material. There were newspaper articles and clippings from books talking about how Hitler had survived World War II. I saw four newspaper clippings from a reputable national newspaper. The first one was dated July 1, 1982. It told the story about how a wanted Nazi war criminal, Manfred Hess, who had been captured by the Mossad, had volunteered the fact that Hitler was alive and living somewhere in South America. The same paper had an article dated July 15, 1982, and this time the story told that Herr Hess had been found hanging in his cell. The next article was dated September 11, 2015. In this article, Maytham al-Tammar, a captured Al-Qaeda leader swore in open court in the United States that he had actually met Hitler in 2008. He claimed if he were released, he would lead the government to him. The final article about al-Tammar was dated September 16, 2015. Apparently, it's not a healthy practice to admit to having seen Hitler. He was found dead in his cell. He too was found having hung himself in his cell. I guess he had been overcome with grief and couldn't handle what he had done. I put the file to the side and sat there shaking my head. I thought I had seen everything, but this file was clearly something new. I analyzed what I had just read. While Hitler had escaped from Germany, there was nothing on this earth that could have kept him for as long as these people were claiming. Perhaps both men had lied and they had met the leader of some secret Nazi organization that had laid dormant for all these years and now planned to rise up and stage a revolution somewhere? They both realized that saying Hitler's name would get them more attention and a lesser sentence even if they were lying, but a nest of Nazi's had been found out. That was the theory that made the most sense. Naturally, they would still own Caesar's Medallion as they had acquired it from Hitler after his death. The two recent deaths of the prisoners really concerned me.

Jesus, I thought. What have I gotten myself into? If this file is on the level, it is absolutely toxic. Assuming Hitler was dead, it looked like Willard or Bobby had stumbled on to some cabal out for no good. The one thing I was sure of even at this early date was that there would be hell to pay one way or another. I tried to think about the nice recovery fee I would be getting when I solved the case. Those thoughts didn't help much. I still felt myself breaking out into a cold sweat.

I picked up the second file that I had found in Willard's safe. The index tab read Burke, Morgan. I took a sip of my coffee before I opened the file and began to read. I was hoping to find something in her file that would impress me. That's not easy to do.

I first looked at a couple of pictures of her. To be sure Morgan Burke was attractive, but there was something about her that wouldn't make her stand out in a person's mind for a long time. I couldn't tell if it was done by design or natural. As I read on in her file, I would learn it was by design.

Morgan was thirty-three and had attended Michigan State University. She had played three years of basketball there before a blown ACL had ended her career. She had majored in international relations and in three languages, Spanish, French, and German. She had graduated with honors, Summa Cum Laude. She was also fluent in Farsi, Pashto, and Dari. The fact that she was in ROTC allowed her to be commissioned as a second lieutenant upon her graduation. That caused me to raise an eyebrow, she had indeed kept herself busy while in school. It was also clear she was gifted in languages. Morgan had been a very busy young lady in college to say the least. My only question about her so far was, is there anything she isn't great at?

I flipped through her service record. After some extensive training, she had been sent to Afghanistan. Morgan had taken combat infantry training as well as spending what seemed like a very short time in language schools. She had done two tours in Afghanistan and had spent eight years in the Army. The duty in Afghanistan went a long way in explaining her proficiency in Pashto and Dari, the two official languages in Afghanistan. I whistled softly to myself. She obviously had a real gift for languages. I was kind of jealous. I had to struggle to get through German for two years while I was in college. I was already pretty impressed with Ms. Burke but would become more so as I read on.

I nodded with approval when I saw the special medals she had won. She had won a Silver Star, a Purple Heart, and a Bronze Star. She also had qualified as expert on the firing range and wore the Combat Infantryman's Badge (3rd Award.) Morgan had certainly kept busy during her tours. I knew the only way you can even receive a Combat Infantryman's Badge was to have seen combat.

I saw she had been promoted to Major in five years. This is virtually unheard of. Someone had their eye on her and it looked like she was going to be on her way to one of the top slots in the Pentagon. I wondered why a person with such a brilliant record had chosen to resign her commission after only eight years? Maybe she would tell me at some point, or perhaps I would figure it out on my own.

About eighty percent of her assignments had been redacted. I had learned from Willard that redacted assignments meant either some type of spy work (read CIA, NSA, or Military Intelligence) or some other type of off the book's operations. Her record was perfect, almost too excellent if such a thing is possible. This gave me pause to think.

While her record was impressive, it did not address the elephant in the room. Why had someone with such a successful career left the Army after only eight years? I doubted it was anything political and there was no indication she had been disabled? Oh well, I was confident that I would the answer to that question later.

Since her leaving the Army, her only job had been as Protocol

Officer in the State Department. Her current post was in England. I smiled to myself, if that position, given her record, did not scream Intelligence Officer, nothing did. I remembered reading Cold War spy novels. The bad guys, the Russians, were always cultural attaches or protocol officers. Some things never change.

Of more immediate concern to me what the question of who Morgan was working for. Would I be able to count on her to help me when the mission became dangerous? It wasn't a question of ability, she had that. It was a question of where her loyalties lay. These were bothersome questions that I would need to have answered. Now that I was done, I returned the files to the safest place I knew of, the safe in my office.

I smiled to myself. Willard had insisted on a diplomatic passport. That told me he expected trouble in Argentina. Have a diplomatic passport to easily be the difference between simply being deported or spending time in an Argentine prison. That cagy old bastard. It wasn't an accident that he had been a very successful Private Investigator. He tried to look ahead and solve problems before they become problems.

Something Bobby had let slip was the fact that the Medallion would have to be studied by some top experts. Why would something as simple as a Medallion need to be studied? It seemed to me that the Medallion was well known, at least in certain circles, all that would be required is to have it verified. That would require a Carbon-14 test and a comparison to the picture that the insurance company had of it. Hardly a long-term project. Was there something above my paygrade that Bobby was withholding from me? I heard a loud rap on the outside door. Just what I didn't want to hear as I was getting ready to call it a day.

I looked at my watch, at 730 PM. I stared out the window in my office and saw the twinkling of the street lights. I reached into my desk and pulled out my Glock-17. Out of instinct, I also reached for a suppressor. I screwed it into the barrel; then I pulled the slide back, making sure I had a round in the chamber. "Prepare for the worst and hope for the best" had been a motto I had lived my life by. With any luck, it was just some confused person who had gotten lost. I carried the pistol at my side as I opened the door to my office and stepped into the reception area. The sensor that controlled the lights in my office turned them off moments after

I left it. I really wanted to go out, get a bite to eat and head home. One of the satellite channels was showing the entire Thin Man movie series. It was one of my favorites and I really didn't want to miss it. Please, I thought, just be some random drunk or lost soul. Nick and Nora await me.

Chapter Five

"The past cannot be changed. The future is yet in your power." Unknown

The pounding on the glass door made a real racket. It stopped once the person at the door saw me. He was a man of indeterminate age and appeared to of medium build. He dressed in a delivery outfit from a local pizza place and was carrying a pizza box. With my free hand, I waved at him and shouted, "Wrong address."

He nodded no. "Isn't this 815 South Illinois?"

I was reasonably safe as all the windows in this building are bulletproof. I eyed the delivery man carefully; something did not seem quite right. I saw he had a Cadillac Escalade with the engine running parked on the street. I could see the exhaust smoking out the pipe of the SUV. He had on what looked like some very expensive shoes on and I caught a glint of gold on his wrist as the streetlight bounced off his wrist. I had delivered pizzas in college. I always wore running shoes and a cheap watch. I owned an expensive one, an Omega Seamaster, but I was always afraid I would lose it in a robbery. Something was really wrong here. I knew the guy could not be the courier that Layne had mentioned. He wasn't arriving until the morning. I thought back to the attack on Willard that had only occurred a couple of days earlier. "What's the phone number on the order?"

"618-555-1212."

"Yes, it is, but I ordered no pizza. Someone is playing a prank on you. Here, I will let you in and you can call the store and get the right address." He didn't appear to be armed, or at least have a weapon in the open and ready for use. However, I suspected he was armed somehow. It was the only thing that made sense. I came to the conclusion that this guy had bad intentions and I had to disable him. That was not happening until I opened the door. I first turned off the alarm, then I reached over, again with my free hand and turned a lock to unlock the door. I motioned him in and turned my back on him for a moment to conceal my pistol. When I heard the bell tinkle, signifying he had indeed pushed the door open, I turned around and fired two rounds. I aimed for his head and sent the first shot right between his eyes. The second shot went through his right eye. I heard a clatter as a what looked like a stun gun fall from his hand and drop to the floor. He slumped to the floor and was dead before he had even realized what happened. If this guy was who I thought he was, he would have to be wearing a bulletproof vest. I quickly checked the body. It verified what I already knew. There were two immediate problems. I needed to get his vehicle off the street before it attracted any attention. The windows were tinted, but I was reasonably sure there was no one inside. People in his line of work typically work alone. I reset the alarm and went outside, taking care to lock the door.

I hopped into his vehicle and drove it to a parking lot in the back of the Agency's building. I glanced over at the passenger seat and saw a doctor's bag. Once I got the vehicle into the Agency parking lot, I turned off the engine and pocketed the keys. I checked the medical kit. There were several scalpels, very sharp hooks, and other implements to make your subject tell you what you want to know. I shivered. I still had work to do, so I got out and then I went back to my office. I began to examine the man much closer. He indeed had been wearing a vest, so my instinct to shoot him in the head, a more difficult shot, to be sure, had been right. The watch had been a Rolex and the shoes looked like some very expensive Italian models. Naturally, he had no ID on him. When I checked under his jacket, I found he had a silenced .22 in a shoulder holster. The .22 is the gun of choice of such diverse groups such as the CIA, La Cosa Nostra, and the Mossad. Once it enters your brain, the bullet really bounces around and does incredible damage. I checked the pizza box and sighed when I saw what was in it. I love pepperoni pizza. It was even still hot. Just my luck. What a waste. I stood up and went back to my office. It seemed prudent not to use my real phone, but a burner to do what I had to do.

I dialed the number on the piece of paper Willard had given me. I waited impatiently as I heard the phone begin to ring. It was answered on the tenth ring. I heard two clicking sounds then for a few seconds, then some hold music.

"Kaplan Cleaning Company," a feminine voice finally answered.

"I need a cleanup at 815 South Illinois in Carbondale, Illinois. I also need a vehicle pick up. It's located behind my building in the parking lot. It's a Cadillac Escalade, black."

I heard a pause, "I am sorry sir, I have no idea what you are talking about. This is a janitorial supply company."

I cursed my own stupidity and then said the code word Willard had written down. I held my breath as I waited for a response.

"Very good. I am assuming you are Mr. Rixey? We heard about what happened to Mr. Bishop. Please send him our condolences. In the future, please use the code word before placing your order."

"Yes, Ma'am."

"You are now using Mr. Bishop's office?"

"Yes, I am."

"You'll find your new code word in the humidor on your desk."

"Yes, Ma'am. Um, do you need me for anything else? Also, if possible, I would like to find out who I shot. The face is in bad shape, may fingerprint him?"

I heard a chuckle on the other end, "Don't teach your grandmother how to suck eggs, son. We will have him printed and with any luck come up with some sort of ID on him. You will find the answer if we can come up with one by the time you open your office tomorrow. It will be on your desk in a plain white envelope/ Now, young man, the best thing you can do is leave and forget this ever happened. You will be getting a bill for cleaning supplies from us. Please pay promptly and thank you for calling Kaplan Cleaning Company."

I nodded to myself and clicked off. I knew there were a few things I needed to do before Kaplan arrived. I didn't want to be here when they got here. These people were professionals and certainly didn't need me here.

I removed the battery from the burner and tossed it in the garbage can. I stepped on the burner crushing it into pieces. I reset the alarm and locked the building. As I stepped outside, I tossed the parts of the phone down a sewer drainage grill. I had holstered my pistol and headed to the back parking lot where my SUV was parked next to the Escalade. I began to shake some as the adrenaline was now beginning to wear off. In my entire time working as a Private Investigator, I had never drawn my pistol in anger, much less killed someone. I didn't feel particularly bad about it. After all, I rationalized, he was planning to kill me. As I headed to the parking lot, I saw a figure looming in the darkness. Fuck, I thought as I reached for my pistol, the guy hadn't been working alone after all. I held it by my side concealing it from view.

Chapter Six

"I don't mind a reasonable amount of trouble." Dashiell Hammett

The figure stumbled toward me as he came of me out of the darkness. I raised my weapon, prepared to fire. Luckily for the figure, I recognized him in the nick of time. I scolded myself and lowered the pistol to my side when I saw who it was. It was a local homeless guy who went by the name of Banner.

I had felt sympathy for Banner. I had Willard look him up one day. Served in Afghanistan, ended up with PTSD. He couldn't adjust in regular society and he fell between the cracks at the VA and eventually lost everything and ended up on the streets. It was another tragic story in a long line of tragic stories about how our country treated those who served it. I tried to help him once, I had gotten him into a rehab program. That lasted about a week and he walked off. I told him if he ever wanted to his act together, I'd help. To help him out, from time to time I would give him small jobs to do around the office. He was a likable guy, even by Ms. Nickels.

"Banner, what the hell you doing lurking around here in the dark?"

"Mr. Rixey, you got something for me? Maybe sweep your office or something?" he asked in a slurred voice. He hiccupped.

I felt my Blood Alcohol Count triple just from smelling his breath. I holstered my pistol and began digging through my pockets for my money clip. I pulled it out of my pocket and peeled off two twenties. "Nothing tonight. Let's call this an advance on the next time I need you to work, fair enough?" as I handed him the twenties. I knew that while Banner was homeless, he still had his pride. He would never accept a direct handout from anyone. By the time, I had another task for him to complete, he would have long since forgotten about the advance.

Thank you, Mr., Rixey. You're a good man really, Banner said as he accepted the two crisp twenties. He waved at me as he stumbled off to who knows where.

Was I a good man? I was beginning to have my doubts. It had been a long day for me and I could feel it was taking its toll on me.

I suddenly stopped, "Man, I am being stupid," I said to the darkness. I took out my phone, turned it on and punched in the security code for the phone. Once the light came on indicating the line was secured, I dialed a number. The phone rang a couple of times and then I heard a click and some whirring noises in the background.

"Umbrella Security."

"Do you know who this is?"

There was a short pause, "Yes sir. Mr. Rixey, what can we do for you?

"Mr. Bishop is in a hospital in Carbondale. He was shot and beaten. I have some very strong concerns about his safety and I will need your best men on his door and anywhere else he goes in the hospital until he is r eady to leave. I need your best and your toughest men guarding him. I am certain he is in great danger. Will that be a problem?"

"Not at all Mr. Rixey. We had heard of his misfortune and stand ready to help. We can have two men there in about twenty minutes. As usual, we will send the bill to the Agency?"

"Somewhat distracted by all that had happened tonight, I paused to get my thoughts back in order, "Oh yes. Quite right. Thank you," I said in a halting manner.

"Not a problem at all, sir. Please have a nice evening."

I switched off and put the phone back in my pocket and headed to my car. I still had time to pick up some take out and then to catch most of the Thin Man movies. I did have a happy thought on my way to my SUV, tomorrow could not possibly be any worse than today.

Chapter Seven

"If you do not change direction, you may end up where you are heading."
Lao Tzu

I woke early the next morning, having spent a restless and dreamless night. I took a shower, got dressed, got a cup of coffee, and enjoyed my first cigar of the day. I logged onto my computer and checked local news and found no mention of dead bodies or stolen cars. I hadn't expected to; I was sure if Willard used them, Kaplan was efficient. I checked my email accounts, nothing of any interest there. Well, I am not being candid. I found I was entitled to 20,000,000 because some family had died in Nigeria. All I had to do was give them my social security number, bank account number, and mother's maiden name and the money was mine. I smiled to myself as I deleted the email. I logged off, grabbed my fedora and brown bomber jacket and was heading for the office.

I got to the office about 730 and parked behind the building. The Escalade was gone, but Ms. Nickels car was there. I walked around to the front of the building and saw the reception area was empty. I heard a buzzer and pushed the door open, hearing the familiar tinkle of the greeting bell. The same signal that had probably saved my life last night.

Ms. Nickels came out of her office. "Good morning, Sir. The usual pot of coffee?"

I nodded, "Yes please." I stole a quick glance around the reception area, no signs remained of what had gone on last night. I sighed in relief. "Did the mail come in yet?" Ms. Nickels?

"No sir, he seems to be running a little late."

I went to my office and saw two items on my desk. The first was a bill from Kaplan for $25,000 and the second was a plain white envelope. I took a seat and then picked up the envelope.

"Mr. Rixey: The man who we found in the office was named George Evan Meyer. We have enclosed a picture of him. Our identification based on his fingerprints is 99.98 percent certain. According to his military file and corroborated with other sources, Mr. Meyer died in a helicopter training exercise in Iraq on June 6, 2013. All we were able to discern that he was in Special Forces. Virtually every assignment he was sent on has been redacted. At this time, we are unable to garner any further information on the person in question. As you are a preferred client, there is no additional charge for this information."

I carefully folded the paper and put it in my pocket.

The report gave me pause for thought. I just killed a guy who had been dead for three years? I thought about the various movies I have seen and the books I had read, I didn't like the conclusion I was rapidly coming to. In those movies and books, the people who supposedly died, but were somehow still alive always worked for large enough organizations that could conceal a death and they were always spies or assassins. Not good. I pocketed the picture and put the folder in my safe. As I stood up, I heard a knock at my door.

"Come."

Ms. Nickels entered with my pot of coffee and set it on a corner of my desk. "Will that be all, Mr. Rixey?"

I held up a copy of the bill from Kaplan for their work last night, "Can you handle this, Ms. Nickels?"

I saw the normally stoic Ms. Nickels, turn pale and saw her body tremble when she saw the bill. She knew what the statement meant. Willard had used their services before. She quickly regained her composure. "Yes, sir. I will have the money wired to their account shortly. Anything else?" When I remained silent, she picked up the bill and walked out of the office. Human nature being what it is, I knew she was dying to know why the Agency was paying off a $25,000 bill to Kaplan. She was too good of an employee to ask why.

I sat at my desk, sipping my coffee and thinking. Just like when I had taken the job here had changed my life, the events of last night had also sent my life on another path. I didn't feel the least bit of guilt for having done what I did. If I hadn't killed Mr. Meyers, I would be dead and the mission would have been likely compromised.

I had things I needed to do but decided to wait for the courier to arrive. I glanced at my watch, time was flying, it was already 930.

Almost on cue, I heard a buzzer, "Yes, Ms. Nickels?"

"Two men here with Secure Courier. I checked their identification and confirmed with a call to their home office. The sender of the package is Mr. Robert Layne. Shall I send them in?"

"Please do."

I heard a knock on my office door. "Come." I looked at my watch, Bobby had been serious about getting me what I needed for the case rather quickly.

The door slowly pushed open and two rather large and serious looking men entered my office. They wore blazers proclaiming; they were employees of Security Couriers. You would have had to have been blind to miss the bulges under each of their blazers.

One of the men approached my desk with a clipboard. "Please sign here, sir."

Usually, I would be reluctant to sign for anything until I had examined it, but considering who it came from and what I expected to be in the parcel, I decided to make an exception. I scribbled my signature on the clipboard.

The second man placed the parcel on my desk and stepped back. "Thank you, gentlemen. You have a good day." I watched them leave.

I started to open the parcel and then stopped. I reached into my desk and pulled out the same wand I had used on Mr. Landry yesterday. I ran it over the box, and much to my delight, no noises or electronic pulses registered on my meter.

I finished opening the parcel and everything was as it was supposed to be. My diplomatic passport, my airline tickets, and $150,000 in crisp one-hundred-dollar bills. I peeled off twenty bills and put them in my money clip. I put everything else in the safe. That task done, I decided it was time to talk to Willard. I had a lot of questions to ask and he was the only one who could really answer them. I reached into the desk and pulled out a portable white noise maker. I hadn't the time to even take off my coat or hat and out of instinct, I felt under my jacket to make sure I had my pistol with me. I walked by Ms. Nickels office and said, "I am going to the hospital to visit Willard. Call me if anything arises. Oh yes, if I have anything scheduled for later on today, please call them with my apologies and reset the appointments? If it something urgent, um, do we have a reliable agency we can refer them to?"

"You had nothing else scheduled for the day other than the security drop. I will inform you if something arises," I heard from behind the door.

I got in my SUV and started it up and headed for the hospital. I decided to call ahead and give them a few minutes' notice. I punched the phone number on the Bluetooth. It rang once.

"Carbondale Hospital."

"Willard Bishop, please. He is or was a patient in ICU."

There was a short pause, followed by a click, a female voice, followed by what seemed to be a panicked response," Who is this?"

"Miller Rixey. I am on the visiting list."

"Oh yes, I remember you. The nice young man who visited Mr. Bishop yesterday." She gulped. "Umm, Mr. Bishop seems to be missing. Is this serious or does he like to wander off?" Also, I noticed the men who had been guarding his room have also vanished."

"Don't do anything until I get there. I am five minutes out." I clicked off and stepped on the gas. I wondered, was there anything else that could go wrong? First the shooting and then what happened to me last night? Now it looks like someone has abducted Willard. I parked in a no-parking zone in front of the hospital and charged into the building. I had to find out what the hell had happened to Willard?

Chapter Eight

"An investment in knowledge pays the best interest." Benjamin Franklin

The nurse who had spoken to me when I was visiting Willard in ICU was waiting at the front desk for me as I exploded through the doors like a crazy man. "I'm so sorry, Mr. Rixey, to have alarmed you. Mr. Bishop snuck out of his room and is in the Atrium Lounge even as we speak." She pointed to a location halfway down the corridor. "Just take this corridor to where you see the two men in suits standing outside. That's the Atrium Lounge."

Somewhat relieved, I could now afford to be gracious, "I understand Nurse, things can happen in big hospitals." I headed down the corridor.

As I neared the room the guards had been standing outside of, I could tell these were some very big and I was guessing rough men. I couldn't say for sure, but I was confident that they were carrying. I wondered where their weapons were as they were dressed in scrubs to blend in with the hospital better. I decided not to ask them and find out. Nothing was proclaiming that they worked for Umbrella Security. Willard had chosen quite well.

"I am here to see Mr. Bishop; my name is Miller Rixey. I believe I am expected."

The guard looked down at what looked like some type of tablet. He looked at what I guessed were pictures and names of those allowed in. When he found mine, he cracked a smile, "Please go right in, sir."

"You realize I have a weapon on me, right?"

"Yes sir, Mr. Bishop said you would be and not to be worried about it. That's why we didn't use a wand on you, now if you please, sir," said the guard that was holding the door open for me. I had a sense that those two men were people I did not want to ever tangle with.

I walked into the lounge and saw Willard sitting in his wheelchair, having an animated discussion with another man who was wearing a lab coat. There was a cloud of smoke over the area of the table as Willard was puffing away on a cigarette.

He saw me, motioned me to the table and then said something to the other man. The man got up, nodding to me, and left the lounge. I heard the door close and turned around to make sure that we were in fact alone.

The man stopped and we shook hands. "Don't worry, Willard will come out of this just like he comes out of everything else. Full of piss and vinegar." He quickly left.

"Miller, come take a seat. Glad to see you," came his booming voice. He reached for another cigarette, Lucky Strike non-filter, and lit it. He sighed in contentment as he took a deep draw.

I grinned at him, "Willard, I am pretty sure that this entire hospital is non-smoking. I think the legislature passed that law back in 2001?"

Willard coughed and in a very raspy voice said, "Son, when you donate the money I did for this lounge, you can be damn sure I made sure it would always allow smoking. I doubt you came here to discuss smoking policy in the People's Republic of Illinois."

I laughed, "You're right about that."

I pulled my white noise maker out of my pocket, set it on the table, and turned it on. Willard nodded when he saw the device.

"What can you tell me about the attack?"

"I was walking through the downtown area heading back to the office. Suddenly a fist appeared out of nowhere and I took collapsed on the sidewalk. I heard a silenced revolver fire once and I felt a burning pain in my side. Then I heard the attacker leave. It was my good luck that at that exact moment, a police car drove by the scene of the attack." He shrugged, "The next thing I remember was waking up in the ICU."

"Do you think you can identify the guy who attacked you. I brought some pictures of some local no goodnicks. Wanna take a try?"

"I'm pretty sure I can; it was dark, but there was plenty of illumination and I never lost consciousness in his presence. I glanced in the direction the punch came from and saw who had hit me. Then I collapsed. I hit my head pretty hard."

I reached into my shirt pocket and pulled out a six-man photo array, "Is the guy who attacked you here?"

Willard pulled out some reading glasses and peered down at the array. "Yes, number four. Hey how did get a picture of that guy? Did he get arrested or something?"

"More like or something. Congratulations, you identified George Evan Meyers, the man I am certain attacked you. He paid me a visit to the Agency last night. It didn't go well for him. Naturally, I had to bring in Kaplan to clean the place and remove his vehicle..."

"Naturally," Willard interrupted.

Anyway, Kaplan identified him through his prints. He was prior military, but was supposed to have died in 2013 in a helicopter crash in Iraq," I said in my best annoyed sounding tone.

Willard whistled and shook his head, "You know I know I should have stayed away from that case, but the money was so good. Now, look at what I got you into."

"I'm a big boy. I decided the $3,000,000 finder's fee plus the $10000 non-refundable retainer and fifty thousand for expenses was a good enough reason for me to take the case."

He sagely nodded, "If I didn't trust your judgment, I would not have even dreamed of retiring."

I turned as I heard the door open. A nurse called in," Remember Mr. Bishop, lunchtime is in twenty minutes. See you then." I turned back to Willard when I saw the door closed.

"Since I was now the boss at the Agency, I took the liberty of going over your caseload and client visitor list. No divorce cases in recent memory and your only client visit in the past two weeks had been Bobby.

When I met Bobby, he was furious; you weren't there. He was sure you had blown him off and left the help as he called it to deal with the problem. You know how I typically run a wand over all my potential clients to make sure they don't have something they shouldn't have on them?"

Willard replied as reached for another cigarette, "I've noticed."

"I picked up some energy pulses coming from a stickpin he wore in his lapel. I got him to remove it, and I put it in a place it wouldn't work. He said it was a family heirloom and in fact, he had worn it at the interview you and he had. My best guess is your attack and my attack are relayed to Caesar's Medallion and Adolf Hitler. I gave him back his pin once we were done and cautioned him to say nothing and behave normally. I am hoping the listeners will simply think it was a malfunction that caused the silence not me discovering it. I think he was more upset that someone had switched pins on him than the fact someone had been eavesdropping on his conversations."

Willard gave a hearty laugh, interrupted by a coughing fit, "Such is the thinking process of the super wealthy."

"Tell me, Willard, what do you think? Am I crazy or on target?"

"Very good, I knew I hired you for a reason. What you have just said makes perfect sense. Along those lines, I am going to assume to read the two files about the assignment that was in the safe?"

"Yeah. That wasn't too hard to figure out. I knew that Layne was meeting you to give you your tickets and passport that you were leaving soon. Given those facts, knowing how you work, I knew you had gotten the research already, it wasn't any great mystery where it was. After Layne left, I decided to check out the contents of the safe. You got a lot of cash and some very nice watches and rings in there," I said with a chuckle.

Willard nodded his head, "I will be taking care of that problem once I'm out of here." He paused for a moment, more importantly, what did you learn from the files? I hope they were helpful. They were not cheap."

"At first, I thought your friends were playing a monstrous joke on you. I found it hard to believe that the US had conspired with Hitler to escape from Germany. The letters sure looked authentic, but...," I shrugged my shoulders. I knew about Operation Paperclip, but I guess I did not realize the full extent of it. The letters were awful and knowing all the Presidents had known about it didn't do much for my confidence in our country.

I saw Willard frown and shake his head.

"My friends while having a sense of humor do not play games when they do their research. They realize that if I am asking them for help, it's serious. You will serve yourself well if you remember that, young man", Willard mildly chastised me.

"Understood. Anyway, I finished the file about Hitler in Argentina and the two newspaper articles combined with the letters changed my thinking. I mean what's the chances that two-people claiming something that is a physical impossibility, Hitler being alive in the 1980s and the 21st century would end up committing suicide by hanging themselves in their cells? My theory was not that had met Hitler, but they had met a leader of a Nazi underground group that is working on some type of revolutionary act. The men had to be killed to nip the Hitler stuff early. This group didn't want to be inadvertently discovered during some bogus investigation.

"Very well thought out. Not exactly the route I used, but we both got to the same destination. What about the file on Morgan Burke?"

"I liked what I read about her. The Army seemed impressed with her, too. I had never heard of anyone making Major in eight years. It's usually ten, if ever. She had a very distinguished record. Two things, I don't understand why she left the Army and I'm guessing she is working some intelligence gig, using her position as a Protocol Officer as cover. I say that because she had quite a few of her assignments redacted. That to me means either intel or some other black bag assignment the government. Nothing else makes any sense. My main concern is who is she really working for when I meet her in Argentina? Is she working for the Nazis, Bobby, the government, or maybe a party we aren't even aware of?"

"Let me put your mind at ease. Morgan works for the government and is very loyal. Loyal to the government that is, not some conspiracy with nefarious plans that is in the government. As for her loyalties toward you, I would trust her one hundred percent."

"Why would that be? I have known you for sixteen years and you trust very few people. Why the exception with her? What sets her apart from most people?" I was baffled. This endorsement was not something Willard Bishop would usually give anyone.

"She is my granddaughter." Willard stood up and we shook hands. "Be careful and best of luck. Please tell her about what happened to me, it might motivate her even more if that's possible. She is a highly motivated young lady to begin with. Now some horrible low salt, low fat, and to tally bland lunch await me."

I stood there dumbfounded and nodded.

He walked me to the door. He headed back to his room and I headed back to the office. I still had plenty of things to catch up on at the office and make sure were taken care of before I left for Buenos Aires. I did not ever want to put Willard in the position where he regretted giving me control of the Agency he had founded and has basically invested his life in.

Chapter Nine

"A journey of a thousand miles begins with a single step." Lao Tzu

Lambert International Airport- St. Louis, Missouri

The shuttle from the hotel dropped me off at the entrance to the airline I would be traveling on for my trip to Argentina. The driver handed me my bag and I passed him a five-dollar bill.

I entered the terminal and looked for my airline and the screening area. I quickly saw a sign proclaiming its presence. I stretched and tried to look as casual as possible as I scanned the crowd, storing as many faces in my memory as I could for future reference. What I did not want to see after my initial scan was the same faces showing up on a reoccurring basis. When that happens in everyday life situations, it doesn't mean much. But this was not a normal life situation. I was working on a radioactive case that could end up affecting history. Seeing the same people over and over again in my position would mean two things. First, who was ever tailing me was sloppy for using the same people. Second, I was, in fact, being tailed. It was early in the morning and I seemed to have caught a break, the line I was heading to did not seem to be too crowded. I headed to the line marked Preapproved TSA Line. I pulled out my TSA ID card as well as my passport. When the attendant saw my TSA card as well as my diplomatic passport, she smiled and pointed to the conveyor belt as I put my bag on it. I made a point to casually scan the crowd of travelers who were going through both checkpoints. When you are working, you can never be too careful. Being able to go through a less busy special lane was a nice change of pace from the harassment and inconvenience that the non-preapproved passengers had to go through. I always wondered why the United States did not follow the Israeli model and make the TSA workers prior military? I heard a beep and my bag was through the scanner. I picked it up and left the scanner area as quickly as I could. I glanced at my watch and saw I still had a few hours left before my flight. I made sure to locate the gate I would be leaving from and then looked for a coffee shop.

As I cleared the screening area, two very grim looking, obvious government types approached me. They were dressed in suits that had obviously come off the rack at some cut-rate men's clothing store. There was a tall man and a short man, the original Mutt and Jeff couple I thought to myself. I knew these guys were going to be trouble. As if on cue, they both reached into their pockets and produced badges. They were from the Department of Homeland Security (DHS). In my experiences in dealing with law enforcement, I have learned it is never a good sign for you when they draw their badges.

I decided to remain outwardly confident and to confront the men first, "Hello sirs. Anything I can do to help you today? Always glad to help my government, "I smarmed.

"Cut the crap, Rixey, we know who you are. Man, I hate guys like you. Why you guys such total jerks? Private dicks are always skirting the law and causing legitimate law enforcement like us problems. You guys are all crooked. Now you're going to come with us and I don't want any lip from you, "the taller one said.

I turned to the other man, the one who seemed to be in charge, "You need to keep your gorilla on a leash. I didn't do anything and I hate being talked down to by a goofball."

I saw the tall man turn a deep crimson as he balled his fists and began to move nearer to me. The shorter man held up his hand, "Jesus, Jack calm down. You can't go around beating up citizens who haven't done anything. I mean what's going to happen when the boss finds out," he whined.

The shorter man turned to me and in the same whining tone of voice said, "There is no need for this conflict. Let's all stay calm. It's quite simple what we want. We are conducting an investigation on some very sensitive matters, and wish for you to answer some questions, Mr. Chambers, who is the U.S. Attorney for this District would like to ask you. It will just be a few minutes. Then you will be on your way. Fair enough?"

I gave a resigned shrug, "Lead the way, sirs."

They led me to an area a short way away from the screening area. On the door, was the sign: Airport Security. The shorter man took his position on the right side of the door and the taller man knocked. I heard a muffled response and the taller man pushed the door open for me and assumed his position on the other side of the door. He silently pointed to me and made a gesture signifying I needed to go in there.

I heard the noises that are typically associated with offices. Phones were ringing, computer printers clicking, and the sound of voices. People were scurrying around, doing whatever people do in office. I could feel an electricity of sorts flowing through the room. I saw a man sitting at a desk with the nameplate of Mr. Chambers and below it, U.S. Attorney. He motioned for me to sit down, pressed a buzzer and a young, thin but curvy brunette, which if I hadn't been working, would have liked to take the time to get to know better, appeared out of nowhere. She slowly sat down in front of a steno machine and a digital recorder. She tested both devices and satisfied they both were working as they should, she sat quietly awaiting further developments.

I saw the man behind the desk point to a seat and I took the hint. He was speaking to one of his assistants and try as I might, I could not hear what Chambers was saying. He gave me an annoyed look as it was apparent I was trying to eavesdrop. The assistant left. I sat there wondering what awaited me.

Chapter Ten

"Life isn't about finding yourself. Life is about creating yourself."
George Bernard Shaw

The man behind the desk turned to face me and cleared his throat, "I am William Chambers, the U.S. Attorney for this area. This woman is Ms. Finch, she is a stenographer, and I will also be recording this interview." the older overweight man said. He nodded and Ms. Finch punched a button on a device on her desk and began typing on her machine.

"Do you feel that you need an attorney present? I ask this bec ause you are not under arrest and are free to leave when you wish. You 're not currently a suspect or a target in an ongoing investigation. I realize the circumstances of this interview may be somewhat unnerving.

I shook my head no.

"Please answer yes or no. We cannot record nods or head shakes."

"I don't need an attorney and I understand completely what you just said. You will have to explain to me why you decided to detain an honest taxpaying citizen who is supposed be enjoying himself while he is on vacation, "I answered gruffly.

"Very good. We are investigating who attacked your boss, Willard Bishop. We believe you have a good idea of who attacked him and why."

"I don't have the foggiest idea."

"Surely, you must have an intelligent and well-reasoned guess? Your reputation for being an excellent detective is well known."

Growing irritated I said, "First, why are the Feds investigating a normal mugging in Carbondale, Illinois. Second, my guess might be excellent and well-reasoned, or it might bc total nonsense. Mrs. Rixey didn't raise any children sappy enough to begin guessing in front of a US Attorney, his stenographer, and while he is being recorded."

"Why not make a guess, unless you have something you are hiding, Mr. Rixey?"

"Everybody has something to hide." I turned to Ms. Finch as I smiled at her, you getting all of this, sweetheart? It's Miller with two ls and my last name is spelled R-I-X-E-Y.

She giggled, blushed ever so slightly, returned my smile, nodded, and kept on working her machine.

"You realize that failing to cooperate in a Federal investigation could be trouble for you, don't you?"

I shrugged, "I don't mind a reasonable amount of trouble."

"Please, Mr. Rixey, there is no need for any hostility. We are working on the same team. Could I have Ms. Finch here get you a cup of coffee?" he pleaded in a whining tone.

As much as I wanted a cup, I shook my head no.

"I'm not sure what team that would be. If we are, why not answer my question about the Feds investigating what looks to me like a common street mugging or robbery attempt?"

Mr. Chambers shook his head, "I'm sorry Mr. Rixey, but that is classified and based on the need to know. I cannot answer that question."

I stood up, "Then we are done here, Mr. Chambers. I assume I am free to go?"

"For now," he said slowly."

I stood up and reached into my pocket for my business card. I handed it to Miss Finch, "Sweetie, here is all of my contact information. If you could please send me a copy of the transcript and the recording, that would be swell."

She replied in a voice that would melt butter, "Mil..., I mean Mr. Rixey." She blushed and looked at Chambers, "I will get both things you requested out as quickly as possible."

I smiled at her, "Thanks, darling. It will be appreciated.:

I then turned back to Chambers, if you want to talk to me again, call my attorney. I assume you know who he is," I said in the angriest tone I could muster. With that, I stormed out of the office. Once outside the office, I began laughing as I walked away from the office. I could see Mutt and Jeff were confused by my behavior. I smiled to myself, another minor victory. I really disliked those types. I quickened my pace as I began my hunt for a coffee shop. There had to be lots of them in an airport. I just can never seem to find one when I need it. I lead a relatively clean life, but I got to have my morning coffee.

I found a coffee shop near the gate. I was going to be using to board my flight. I was pleasantly surprised to see only one person in line ahead of me. These places always seem busy, especially at this time of the morning. I looked around again and was happy to see no one that I had seen in the earlier group of travelers at the check-in lanes. That did not mean I wasn't being followed, but what I didn't see was a good sign.

I approached the counter and was greeted by a very cheerful clerk. She looked like she was in her twenties, medium build, and short blonde hair. I ordered a large iced latte, one of my weaknesses and a local newspaper. The woman made my order quickly enough but fumbled with the paper as she handed it to me. I thanked her, dropped some tip money in the jar, and went to find a secluded table. As I sipped my drink, I checked for voicemails and texts and found out I had none of either. I switched my phone off and then opened the paper to the sports section. A piece of paper fluttered out of the paper as I opened it and landed on the table. I shrugged, thinking it was merely an ad insert. The side facing up was blank. Being naturally curious, I turned it over and read it.

"You are most certainly being followed. Beware. S/ W."

After reading the note, I admit I was more than a little surprised. Surprised at the content and surprised in the manner I had received it. I looked back at the counter and saw the clerk who had waited on me had disappeared. I put my paper in my bag and walked back over to the counter. I thought nothing of that occurring, in fast foods, people frequently change positions I thought nothing of that happening, but I did have a few quest ions I wanted to ask her. There was no one waiting to be served, so my timing seemed perfect. I slid up to counter and returned the clerk 's smile with one of my own.

I broke the silence with the clerk, "May I speak to the manager, please?"

"Is there a problem?"

"No. Not at all. I had a question for him or her."

She yelled back, "Hey Chris, someone wants to see you." She turned back toward me and smiled sweetly, "He will be up here in a moment."

I nodded my thanks.

Shortly, a young, thin, wiry man, with an air of self-importance that some people get from wearing a manager name tag, a pocked marked face, a shaved head, and one of those pencil mustaches I do so hate, came to the counter.

Clearly annoyed at having been taken away from whatever important tasks people like this do, he asked, "May I help you?"

"Yes, I got really great service from one of your clerks. I wanted to leave a favorable comment card for her. She looked to me to be about twenty or so, medium build, and short blonde hair. I did not catch her name."

Another customer had walked up to the kiosk and I stepped aside. I quickly glanced at her. She was medium height and build, a blonde and well dressed. More importantly, I had not seen her before. I stood there, waiting for an answer from the manager.

"You must be confused, sir. We don't have anyone who works at this kiosk who matches that description. The clerk on duty is the only I have scheduled until noon." He pointed to the clerk, "Dolly has been here all morning, haven't you?"

"Yes, Bruce. Since 5:00 AM."

"See, must have been another kiosk. It's easy to be confused here," he said in his most polite and condescending manner. "If there is nothing else, I need to get back to work." He turned on his heel and stomped off to whatever important task awaited him.

I thanked him back for his time. I realized there was nothing more to be gained by further questioning of Bruce and Dolly, so I left. I looked at my watch. I still had plenty of time to kill before my flight left, so I returned to the table and began drinking my coffee and reading my paper.

Sometime later, I heard a call for my flight. I repacked my bag and headed toward the departure lounge, checking my surroundings as I walked there. I noticed a side door, located by the gate open. I saw the two DHS agents I had met earlier, escorting a gurney out of from wherever they had come from. Three EMT's seemed to be working on the person on the stretcher, the body on the gurney was the clerk who had waited on me. I thought this is a horrible sign. Someone had discovered what the clerk had done and had now taken retribution out on her. This was not a good sign at all.

I moved with purpose, making sure I didn't run or do something else to attract attention, toward the area the flight attendant was checking boarding passes. I handed the Boarding Agent my ticket and she smiled as she saw my first-class ticket. She looked at it and scanned it. When the light indicator flipped to green, she said, "Hope you enjoy your flight Mr. Rixey. We will be serving a snack about an hour after we take off. If there is anything, anything at all that you need, please let me know."

Peering at her nameplate, I replied, "Thank you, Ms. Kingery."

She nodded at me and pointed toward first class. I followed the direction of her finger and soon found first class.

I found my seat, placed my bag under my seat and then buckled up. I looked around first class and saw it was almost empty. I sat back and relaxed.

Chapter Eleven

"I was taught that the way of progress is neither swift nor easy."
Marie Curie

So far so good, I didn't notice any familiar faces as I took my seat. I remembered the adage that had helped carry me through my career so far; never lie to yourself. The attack on Willard, the attempted attack on me, the interview with that blowhard, Chambers, combined with the note I was passed from the so-called clerk at the kiosk were factors in the honest analysis that I was in great danger. The clerk's note had gained instant credibility once I saw her being carried out on a stretcher. I suppose she could have had an accident, but she somehow got behind the kiosk counter, slipped me a note, and then vanished. Shortly later, she had been severely beaten or perhaps worse. Enough thinking for now I thought. There would be time to hash this out when I got to speak to Willard once I arrived in Atlanta. I stretched for a moment in my all too comfortable seat and then reached for my bag and took out a book about Nazi Germany that I had purchased at a Carbondale retailer. I quickly turned my attention to the book.

As I opened the book, I heard an announcement over the loudspeaker in Spanish and English: "This is your flight captain speaking. We will be taking off on this flight to Buenos Aires shortly. Please make sure you're buckled in and please keep all electronic devices off until you are told they are permitted. We will be making a stop in Atlanta, which will have a holdover of two hours. After that, we will continue to Ministro Pistani International in Buenos Aires. Our estimated arrival time will be

1230 AM Buenos Aires time, which is three hours later than St. Louis time. Please pay proper attention to the flight attendants when they instruct you on emergency procedures. Thank you for flying with us."

I looked at my watch and inwardly groaned. It read 8:58 AM. I felt the vibrations of the engines and when I looked out my window, I saw the jet as it moved to its takeoff position on the runaway. Moments later, we were airborne.

I heard the speakers come to life again as the flight attendants began addressing emergency and safety procedures. Like most experience travelers, I quickly tuned them out. I had heard the same lecture numerous times.

I took a deep breath and did my best to relax. I knew to get tense and worrying myself into an ulcer was not going to help me solve the case as to the Medallion or stay alive in Argentina.

I heard the speakers come to life again: "We will be landing in Atlanta in thirty minutes. The stay will be for two hours to allow time for refueling and other tasks. For those continuing to Buenos Aires, please make sure you have your boarding passes in order. If you go past the TSA checkpoints, you will be required to submit to another search."

I was about a third of the way through the book but really hadn't learned anything new. It talked about Hitler's escape from Germany and some of the groups that had been complicit in his flight such as the American government, the Vatican, and a group called ODESSA. ODESSA which was a German abbreviation for "Former Members of the SS," oversaw the distribution of papers and money for lower to midrange Nazis who made it to Argentina. The upper-level Nazis such as Hitler or Bormann had enough wealth that they had little need for that group.

As a devotee of The History Channel, sometimes called "The Hitler Channel" by wags, I had learned more than I ever needed to know about the Nazis. I was grateful that it helped me pass some time and placed the book in my bag and buckled my seatbelt for landing.

One of the flight attendants stopped by my seat, "Mr. Rixey, there is going to be a roughly two-hour layover in Atlanta. Will you be deplaning when we reach Atlanta?" she asked.

I looked up in surprise, "I thought everyone had to get off at landing. I mean isn't that the normal procedure on these types of flights?"

I saw a couple of passengers in first class get up. They seemed to be heading toward the exit.

She smiled, "No Mr. Rixey, our special passengers are allowed to stay aboard as this is the same plane that you will be taking to Argentina. If you choose to stay aboard, you will have an opportunity to order breakfast. Your television will work just fine and we will keep it from getting too stuffy in here by keeping the air conditioning running. How does that sound to you, sir?"

"I'll be getting off. I could really use a cigar about now. I assume you have smoking areas for your special passengers?" I asked.

"Yes. We love to make our special passengers like yourself feel treasured. Just look for the First-Class Lounge for this airline. It is quite close to where you will be deplaning and then getting back on board. I will check back to see if you stayed on or left. If you are still here, I am sure we will be able to find something for you. Now, Mr. Rixey, if there is nothing else, I have to go tend to my other passengers," she said with a smile as she walked away to tend to the other first-class passengers. She swayed as she walked away. Just my luck, I thought.

Chapter Twelve

"If you tell the truth, you don't have to remember anything."
Mark Twain

I quickly found the lounge and pushed the door open. I pushed the door open and looked around the room. It was spacious. There were about a dozen tables, each surrounded by chairs, what looked like a hardwood bar, and a wide variety of plants scattered around the room. The light in the room was provided by a skylight during the day. As the weather was overcast, the lights had been turned on. I saw maybe a half dozen people sitting at the bar. I raised my hand and caught the bartender's attention. She seemed like a friendly sort of person. Perhaps a little overweight, but still attractive. I guessed her maybe a college student in her early twenties. She quickly approached where I had been standing, "Good morning sir, is there anything I can get you?" She handed me a menu.

I quickly read the menu and then I looked at my watch. It was still shy of 8:00. "How about a cup of coffee. Three creams and three sugars if you please."

I looked around the room looking for the smoking lounge door and soon found it. The bartender returned with my coffee.

"How much do I owe you?" I asked.

"No charge, sir. It comes with your ticket."

I fumbled for some bills and laid a five spot on the bar. "Thanks," I said. I turned away and headed for the smoking lounge.

The lounge was empty. I took a table in the corner. After taking a sip of my coffee, I opened my bag and pulled out my traveling humidor and opened it. I pulled out a cigar, smelled it and lightly squeezed it. Perfection. I took out my clipper and cut the end off, placed it in my mouth and lit it.

I fished around in my jacket pocket and pulled out my cell phone. On the surface, it just looked like a cheap phone. That was the effect I was looking for. The phone had some features that were not apparent to the average onlooker. It was encrypted. Even if someone were in the position to listen in on my conversation, they would hear nothing but garbled noise. It was also impossible to track when I called someone. My messages would be bounced all over the world by a satellite that was owned by my phone service. My phone also could not be tracked. The annoying GPS device had long since been removed. The last feature was when I pressed a special key, two electrically charged prongs would appear in the top of the phone. If you stuck the prongs into someone, they wouldn't forget it. There was not enough power to kill, but enough to make the target regret you had stuck it in them. I had used it that way once as a test and had seen the results. It wasn't pretty. I turned the phone on and punched in the security code. The screen came to life. A few moments later, the secured light began flashing. Once it stopped flashing, I knew the phone was now secure and ready for relatively safe use.

I checked my phone for voicemails or messages, there were none. I then dialed my office. Ms. Nickels answered on the first ring, "Good morning Miller. How has your trip been so far?"

"So far, so good. I am calling from Atlanta. My flight from here leaves in about ninety minutes. How's Willard doing? Any updates? Anything I need to know about?"

"You have a special appointment next week. If something comes up and you have a chance, please call me and I will reschedule. We had an insurance case come in, I referred it to another agency as you will be much too busy to handle it. Willard is doing fine and expects to be released shortly. Also, before you ask, nothing from Mr. Layne. That should bring you up to date on Agency business. Anything else?"

"No, sounds good. I will check my email in case something important arises when I get to Buenos Aires. Go ahead and take the rest of the day off, you have been working much too hard lately."

"Thank you, Mr. Rixey, I will. It's very greatly appreciated. Please be careful, I would hate to work for a new boss."

"Don't worry, I will," I reassured her as I clicked off. I saw no reason to alarm her with the happenings of today.

My next call was to Willard.

He picked up on the first ring. "Hello, Miller, how has your trip been so far?"

"Well, to be honest, I've had better trips. Before I flew out of St. Louis, I got dragged into an interview room and got to speak to a Mr. Chambers. I guess he is the US Attorney for our district. He sounded like a total blowhard. You and I know what happened, but how could they have discovered a nexus to let the Feds get involved in investigating the attack on you? I mean it looks like a mugging or armed robbery gone bad."

If anything, it tells me Mr. Layne has a massive security problem. I would keep him in the dark as long as possible. If the Medallion is simply a historical artifact, I don't understand their involvement. If there is some type of power that comes from the Medallion, now we are getting into an area that would involve national security. You are fortunate, Chambers is as dumb as a box of rocks. I knew you had been dragged off, I had two, umm, let's say, friends, following you. Don't feel bad if you didn't pick up on them. They are former intel agents and were switching off. They told me you weren't kept too long and I had faith in you to keep your wits about you. They said you got into it with a couple of DHS agents. You need to keep your cool, young man."

"I do my best, but sometimes, you know, you have to send a message you aren't going to stand there and take their crap."

"I understand, but keep in mind you are a professional. I also realize we are all human."

"Did your friends tell you about what happened at the coffee kiosk?"

"No. I sent my friends home after I heard you emerged from the interview room."

"Someone posing as a clerk passed me a note hidden in a newspaper. I was guessing she was one of your friends. Female, early twenties, medium build, short blonde hair. Sound familiar?"

There was a long pause. "No idea."

"You might want to look into it. When I went back to the counter, she was long gone and no one had heard of her. Then as I was boarding, she was being wheeled out on a gurney that was escorted by the two DHS agents who had met me at the screening area. Three EMTs were working on her. I don't know what happened to her."

"Don't be afraid to rely on Morgan. She is a very competent young lady and this isn't a proud grandfather speaking."

"Okay Willard, I am switching off. Take care."

I sipped my coffee and began to reanalyze all had occurred so far in this case. The interview with Layne and the files I had read in the office, combined with the attack on Willard, the attempted attack on me, and what I had seen this morning had brought the whole Caesar's Medallion story into clear focus. I was now sure that Caesar's Medallion was somehow tied into some giant conspiracy. The question remained, what was the plot? Was I missing something? Sure, the Medallion was a valuable, possibly priceless artifact, but it seemed like people were going to a lot of trouble to make sure the Medallion was not going to be recovered. I tried to narrow my thinking just to the Hitler in Argentina file and my interview with Layne. I in the lounge deep it thought. It came to me like a thunderbolt, as insane as it sounded, the Medallion had some kind of mysterious power? That was why Layne had been so insistent on the fact that the Medallion needed to be studied. That would also explain why the interview with the feds. The government also realized there was some sort of power attached to the Medallion, and being our government needed to get their lunch hooks into it. The government could not be seen to be officially involved, so send someone not connected with the government to find it. Thus, enters The Bishop Detective Agency! Miller Rixey, I thought, you are a pure genius.

I looked up at a digital display that announced arrivals and departures and saw I still had thirty minutes before I had to report to the gate. I finished my coffee and decided to get one more when the door to the lounge swung open. I saw a very old man, if I had to guess, I would put him in his seventies. He stood around 5'10 and weighed maybe 175 to 190. It was hard to tell his weight as he wore on a black trench coat. Even though he was wearing a black fedora, He wore what looked like steel rim glasses and used a cane to help him walk more quickly with his limp. I nodded to him as I walked by him on my way back to the bar. His shaving lotion seemed almost toxic. I coughed as I walked by him.

"Herr Rixey, do you have a moment?" he asked in a thick German accent. His breathing was labored and he took a seat at the first available table in the smoking lounge. He rested his cane on a chair.

"Not especially, I'm kind of in a hurry, what did you need?" I stood there looking at him, attempting to give my best very annoyed look. It wasn't hard to look annoyed, as I really was. I could tell my comments had made little or no impact on the stranger.

He slowly reached into his jacket pocket, I gripped my phone as since I was traveling, I had no real weapon, "Mr. Rixey, it has come to our attention you are traveling to Argentina. Is that correct?" he asked.

"That's really no one's business but mine. Do you need anything else? Get to the point."

He handed me a thick envelope, "May I suggest you take this envelope and enjoy a few days in Argentina with the lovely young lady you are supposed to meet and then return home."

I felt the envelope. It was two inches thick and I was guessing was filled with hundred-dollar bills. I shrugged, "Sorry sir. I have a previous commitment and you never gave me your name. This is very generous of you to offer me an envelope full of cash, but I cannot accept it. You have me confused with someone else." I handed the envelope back to him. I tapped my watch crystal twice to emphasize my annoyance and how I was in a hurry. What he could not have realized was one of the things my watch did function as a camera. I didn't say cheese, but I had quickly taken two very clear pictures of him. "If there is nothing else, I need to get another cup of coffee and then get back to the departure gate for my flight," I said with a tone of exasperation.

The man smiled coldly, "My name Herr Steele. We know who you are and what you are doing. Might I add, you are a very competent operator. My group would most certainly wish to retain you if you were free. You will find that your life will be much healthier and happier for you if you accept the envelope and my friendly advice. Argentina can be a dangerous country. Many accidents can occur. It would be too bad if you had one."

He broke into a coughing fit last lasted for a minute or so.

Waiting for Steele to quit coughing, I adjusted my fedora and nodded. "I appreciate the advice, Herr Steele." I looked at my watch. "None the less, you have me confused with someone else. I hope you find who you are looking for. I must be going. Have a good day." I nodded to him as I walked back to my table and picked up my bag.

When I turned around, Herr Steele had left. The envelope rested on a table. I looked around and decided to pick it up. I stuffed it in an inner pocket of my jacket. I really didn't want to leave something like that laying around for anyone to pick up. I wanted to be able to return it to Herr Steele. I also knew that with my Diplomatic Passport, I was unlikely to be searched when I arrived in Buenos Aires. The last thing I needed was to stand for a frisk at customs in Buenos Aires and be discovered to be carrying a large amount of American currency. That would raise some difficult questions that I was not prepared to answer and or a quick flight back to the US. The Diplomatic Passport help avoid all those problems. The envelope would be safe with me.

At that point, I decided to forgo my second cup of coffee and headed for the gate to board the continuation of my flight to Argentina.

Chapter Thirteen

"A wonderful fact to reflect upon, that every human creature is constituted to be that profound secret and mystery to every other."
Charles Dickens

As I left the lounge, I checked to see if Herr Steele as he called himself, was still in the lounge. He wasn't. I had some questions I needed answered pretty quickly. How was Steele able to find me? How did Steele even know what I was working on? I felt like people were selling tickets to what was supposed to be a secret mission. Only one person could help me. I walked to a tier of seats that was currently empty and pulled out my phone and turned it on. I punched in my security code and waited for secured light to flicker on. Once again, I noticed no voicemails or messages waiting for my attention. Once the secured light flickered on, I dialed Willard's number.

"Hello Miller," Willard's voice boomed over my handset.

"It sure looks like people know what my plans are. Since I last talked to you, I have been approached by a man calling himself Herr Steele. He knew of my plans to go to Argentina. He even knew I was going to meet a lovely young lady down there. That had to be Morgan." I paused waiting to hear what Willard's reaction was going to be. When I heard no response, I continued.

"He offered me a thick envelope to simply spend a few days in Argentina and then return home. I am reasonably certain he is working for someone and judging by his accent is a German national. I need to find out who he is and who he is working for? Even though I didn't think I needed to, I took all the necessary precautions I making sure I was not being followed. Then this guy shows up in an airport lounge. He seemed to know who I was and what my business was. I paused, "I am sending you a picture of him, do you recognize him at all?" I pulled out a pin on my watch and set the time to 1:00. I heard a couple of clicks and then saw a sent message. I pushed the pin back in and reset the time.

"I just received your picture of him. That watch takes some might nice pictures, doesn't it? Seriously though, I idea who he is. As you can tell from the intelligence I you read, there are a lot of major players that had been involved. A friend of mine has access to the largest face recognition program in the word. With any luck, I will have an answer for you when you arrive in Buenos Aires. Miller, please be very careful. The current government has no interest in the story ever coming to light. It would be an embarrassment to a lot of people if word got out about our deal with Hitler. Even if they weren't involved with the deal, it could be a disaster to their family's legacy. You are probably in even greater danger if people are contacting you and offer bribes. You know, no one would think any less of you if you simply abandoned the assignment. I have done that before on some occasions."

"Can't do it. I hate these people for what they did to you and tried to do to me. I won't allow myself to be bullied. Willard, I got to go. They are announcing first class boarding for my flight. I'll show the picture to Morgan and see if she has any idea who it is. And, before you say it, Willard, I will be cautious. I will also check my email, once I get to my room. Anything else? Hearing no answer, I switched off and headed to the gate.

I got to the gate just as first-class boarding began. I flashed my boarding pass at the attendant and she nodded. I found my old seat and stored my bag under my seat. I decided that no matter what danger I might be in once I arrived in Argentina, nothing was going to happen on the plane. I might as well relax while I could. My instincts told me that once I hit Argentina, there wouldn't be much time to relax.

"Did you have a good time in Atlanta, Mr. Rixey?"

I looked up though only out of courtesy. I knew who the speaker was, "Yes Ms. Dinisi, everything was fine. Thank you."

I opened my book about the Nazis in Argentina and continued reading. I pressed my easting control to the maximum still sitting level. I didn't want to fall asleep just yet, I wanted to make sure I finished my book. While I had not learned much from the book, I was hoping that the book would become somehow a pearl of wisdom that may have been overlooked by Willard and his researchers. It turned out I was right. What I read in this book was the key to unraveling this case.

Chapter Fourteen

"The only thing necessary for the triumph of evil is for good men to do nothing." Edmund Burke

After the plane reached cruising altitude, the voice of the captain informed us that we would be landing in Buenos Aires at 1:00am Buenos Aires time, which is three hours ahead of Atlanta time. I adjusted my watch and found a comfortable position in my sear.

My inflight reading material, "Nazis in Argentina," discussed Eva Peron as a major player in the Nazi settlement of Argentina. People really considered her to be the ruler of Argentina, but the time for female chief executives of countries had not come yet.

She handled the delicate negotiations with Martin Bormann, ODESSA, and lesser groups and individuals. Translation: She was responsible for collecting the huge bribes that made sure the Nazis could live in Argentina undisturbed. Perhaps she got a little too enthusiastic in her work as she took a lot more than the bribe amount negotiated. This led to her premature death in 1952 as well as the deaths of two other of her family members. While the official cause of death for her was listed as cancer, the author dismisses that cause out of hand. I thought to myself, she should have known better than to mess with those people. They were bad actors. But greed is a terrible thing and everyone thinks they are bulletproof at that age.

The purpose of ODESSA, which was a German anachronism for "Former Members of the SS," was to provide escape routes, documents, and cash for fleeing SS members either shortly before the end of WWII or soon after. The group was efficient and ruthless the author said. No real surprise there I thought.

Near the end of the chapter dedicated to Eva Peron, I came across an interesting section about her burial.

"After the odyssey, which saw her remains moved around for more than two decades, the Argentine government allowed her to be buried in her family's burial plot in 1978. The plot was located in La Recoleta Cemetery which was established in Buenos Aires.

The tomb was built by a company that specialized in building bank vaults and other objects that required some level of security. The monument, according to the company, was built so solidly, they guaranteed that no one could ever break in and that it would withstand a nuclear attack. Security experts from the Argentine government kept an eye on the construction of the vault. They did not want anything embarrassing happening. Rumor had it that the design of the vault was on the upper level a marble floor had a trap door that led to another room that contained two empty coffins. Both coffins were supposedly empty. The coffins concealed another trap door that apparently led to the final level of the vault where Eva Peron rested for eternity in a glass coffin. The only way to access the building was with a key that had been given to Eva's sister. The location of the key and her sister remain a mystery. As far as anyone knew, the tomb had not been entered since it was initially sealed in 1978.

I looked at some pictures of the monument. The front was covered with various plaques, some rather plain and some rather ornate. The front door was festooned with flowers. It looked quite befitting a burial vault of someone of her rank in society. The back was as one would expect, plain except for one small carving. I took out my magnifying glass and studied the engraving. It was a copy of Caesar's Medallion.

I closed the book and sat back in my seat to digest what I had read. I had heard about the crazy stories that the Argentine government was afraid of Eva escaping from her vault and leading the people in a revolution that would return her to power. I snorted in disbelief. Maybe the peasants would believe this; I had a hard time finding the government also did. No, there had to be some reason for the enhanced security and the Argentine involvement in the building procedure. I might not have even given Peron's grave another thought, but the carving bothered me. I knew that none in Argentina, except for Nazis had any idea of the significance of the carving. One thing I knew for sure, Morgan and I were going to be taking a visit to the La Recoleta Cemetery as soon as it was feasible. There had to be a reason for the carving.

I closed my eyes and was woken by an apologetic flight attendant who asked if I wanted something to eat for brunch. I ordered something light as I don't like flying on a full stomach. I observed her as she sauntered away. She was tall, had a great build, and had blonde hair tied into a severe bun.

She quickly returned with my order. "Here you go, sir," she said with a smile. "Do you visit Argentina often?"

"No, this is my first trip."

"Oh, you must let me show you around. I just love Buenos Aires. It can be most fascinating if you allow someone such as myself to show you around town. There are many interesting places and sights to see."

Just my luck I thought, I am on a case and now a drop-dead gorgeous woman wants to show me the sights. I eyed her closer and saw her nameplate read Ms. Dinisi and that she was a supervisor. "I'm really sorry, I have to meet some friends down there. Maybe something good will happen and I will be able to get away early."

She pulled a card out of her pocket and scribbled something on it and handed it to me. It had her name, phone number, and the hotel she would be staying at. "I will be there for a week, she cooed. I sat in deep regret as I saw her sway her hips as she made her way down the aisle to tend to the other flyers.

A nudge on my shoulder woke me. I had no idea how long I had been sleeping since brunch and the movie. I blinked a couple of time to focus my eyes. They focused on a harried middle-aged, slightly overweight, and balding man approached me. "Miller Rixey?"

I nodded, "That would be me."

"Please show me some ID to verify, Mr. Rixey."

I reached into my shirt pocket and pulled out my passport. He glanced at the picture briefly, nodded, and handed me a folded over piece of paper. He then returned to the cockpit.

I unfolded the note and saw a series of two-digit numbers. I thought for a moment and then reached under my seat for my bag. I fished through one of the side pockets and pulled out a plastic case with a five-wheeled device. It was called a Mexican Army Cipher Disk. It had five disks that will convert two-digit numbers into letters to translate a message and the process is reversed if you wish to send a message. It was very state of the art about one hundred years in the past. Willard loved items like this. Its value was in its obscurity. It was difficult to break without a good computer as it has 450,000 different possible key combinations. It was old and it was primitive and as Willard was fond of saying, it cannot be hacked.

I set the disk on my table and began trying to decode the message. What I saw did not make me very happy. "S-T-E-E-L-E F-M-R C-O-L S-T-A-S-I."

I sat back and sighed. Herr Steele was a former Colonel in the STATSI, the secret police of what used to be East Germany. The STASI was almost as brutal as the KGB. One did not make it to Colonel in the STASI without being intelligent and ruthless. By the time East Germany collapsed and the STASI was disbanded they had left a large collection of bodies behind as well as a large collection of enemies. I needed to be at my best to deal with a man like him.

I put the disk back in my bag and pulped the message. I sat back and did my best to go to sleep, but it wasn't happening. I had too much on my mind.

As Ms. Dinisi walked by, I waved my hand to catch her attention. She returned a smile. "Can you get me a cup of coffee with lots of cream and sugar in it."

"Not a problem, Mr. Rixey. I will get that for you right away."

She returned with my coffee and I thanked her. I put my earphones on and began channel surfing. The news was depressing. That is to say, the news had degenerated into something that no longer seemed like news anymore, at least to me.

A group of third-rate actors was demanding martial law be instituted. Another topic of import was a battle going on at a west coast school about the failure to use proper pronouns when referring to a person's gender. Some other students on the east coast were demanding the

American flag be replaced as it was a symbol of racism and imperialism. We focus on the on issues and ignore issues like gun confiscation, our country spying on honest citizens, and people demanding things they did not understand such as martial law.

I felt the plane hit the landing field with a jolt. I had fallen asleep after all. It hadn't been much, but I felt better. The aircraft taxied for five minutes and stopped. I grabbed my bag and headed toward the exit. Ms. Dinisi gave me another huge smile as she stood at the exit for first class. "Do you have any checked luggage, Mr. Rixey?"

"No. Just this bag."

"You were asleep when we announced the deplaning instructions. Just turn to the left once you leave the gate follow the yellow line and that will take you straight to passport control.

"Thanks. I appreciate everything you did for me. It made my flight much more pleasant." I smiled at her.

"I really hope we can meet up again, Mr. Rixey. Please enjoy your time in Buenos Aires. Don't hesitate to call me if you need anything, anything at all."

I nodded, "I got your information in my wallet. I'll do my best to take you up on your generous offer. I am sure what you told me about Buenos Aires is true, "I said with a smile.

I stepped off the plane and walked down the jetway. I followed her directions and was soon at passport control.

"Business or pleasure?" a very bored uniformed agent asked.

"Pleasure."

"Anything to declare?"

"No."

I heard the sound of the stamp validating my passport." Please enjoy your stay in Argentina, Mr. Rixey." He turned to the next person in line, "Step up please." Once I had cleared passport control, I reached into my pocket and placed five one-hundred-dollar bills inside my passport. Be prepared is a way of life. I knew how things worked south of the border.

I heard a familiar coughing and wheezing sound behind me. I already knew who it was. I turned to see Herr Steele standing there, clutching his cane. He grinned at me, but there was no warmth in the grin.

He slowly started to approach me. He was being followed by two strapping Aryan types. They were completely silent and showed no emotion as they tagged behind Herr Steele. Real master race types. I thought. I stood there waiting for them.

This was not the reception I had been hoping for upon my arrival. I was so hoping to never see Herr Steele again, that was not to be. Like is full of annoying problems, people, and situations. Rightly or wrongly, we are ultimately judged by how we handle ourselves in these instances. I was going to handle this well.

Chapter Fifteen

"God does nothing except in response to believing prayer." John Wesley

Herr Steele approached me flanked by his two bodyguards. "Herr Rixey, I overheard your declaration at passport control. I wish to compliment you on your wise decision...", his diatribe interrupted by an outbreak of coughing and wheezing. I saw him start to stumble, but caught himself with his cane.

I thumbed in the direction of the two bodyguards, "What's with Hans and Fritz. You were able to handle meeting me alone in Atlanta; why the change? I bet your master doesn't let you go out by yourself anymore, does he?

Steele turned crimson, I could see flecks of foam coming from his mouth, and his body shook badly, "Herr Rixey, you would do well to remember I work for no one. No one you hear," he screamed.

At that point, his two bodyguards began to approach me. I knew I wasn't going to like this. They were both well past six feet tall and if they had an ounce of body fat on them, it would be the first. I guessed them for steroid abusers. They were dressed in paramilitary uniforms and wore black well-polished jackboots that ran to their knees. I reached into my pocket for my cell phone. If they wanted to hurt me, I was going to return the favor. I really hated being without a pistol in these types of situations. I had my hand on the button that would activate the Taser. While I didn't have the slightest doubt that Steele would order a beat down on me in an instant, he did not seem like the person who wanted to cause a real public scene. So far, it had been little more than raised voices.

Steele turned to them, made a hand gesture and said something to them in German. The only word I could pick out of the conversation was *nein*. They stopped. I breathed a sigh of relief. Even with my Taser, these guys were probably better fighters and had me by fifty pounds and twelve years.

Steele struggled to regain his composure. He glowered at me, "Herr Rixey, you seek to provoke me with your evil methods. You will lose in the long run as I have superior willpower and am much smarter than you. You will do well to remember that." He had another coughing fit.

I made a split-second decision not to mention to Steele that I knew about his past. It might have been a temporary childish victory and gotten him angrier, but that was something better saved for when it could really matter.

"Herr Steele, I suggest you see a physician. You don't look or sound too well."

He raised his cane, "Herr Rixey, you need to be much more concerned about your own health. I have a feeling the next time we meet, it will not be in a public forum such as this airport."

He then turned to his two bodyguards and said something to them. They marched right in front of me on their way out of the airport terminal. I kept an eye on them as I saw them leave the building.

Two uniformed men approached me, luckily for me, one of them spoke English. "*Señor*, we have had complaints about you and the older gentleman. It seems your discussion got very loud.

Why hadn't they come up while Herr Steele was there, oh well I thought, best to end this right now. I glanced at his insignias on his shirt collar. "Colonel, I am so very sorry about the disturbance. Please be assured it won't happen again. "I handed him my diplomatic passport. There was the proper amount of squeeze in it, as I had the foresight to slip some money inside it.

He smiled at me as he looked at my passport "Señor, I am but a humble Major in this country. I am only wanting to preserve order and security here. Thank you for your apology. Please enjoy your stay here in our beautiful country." He returned my passport; I did not want him to feel threatened or disgraced, I stuffed it back in my pocket with looking to see if he had taken the money. The best way to get into a jam is to make any statement or gesture that threatens the honesty of a government employee, whether he is a crook or not. I nodded and we went our way.

I walked with purpose to the front of the air terminal. No, I wasn't attempting to follow Herr Steele, but I was supposed to meet my contact, Morgan Burke, in a twenty-four-hour restaurant that was located just inside the terminal. I glanced to my right and saw a well-lit sign El Diner del Aeropuerto: Siempre Abierto. My Spanish is a little weak, but even I could figure out what the sign meant. I pushed the door open and was greeted by the sounds of voices speaking in many languages, the clatter of dishes, and the usual sights and sounds that are associated with busy restaurants. A hostess welcomed me and I did my best to overcome the language barrier. She obviously had a better grasp of English than I did of Spanish. The diner was packed even at this odd hour and it took a few minutes of walking around before I spotted Morgan Burke. She stood out in this crowd. I already knew what she looked like from a file picture, but that picture did not do her justice. Her pale skin seemed almost to glow and her long red hair was tied in a ponytail. She wore a baseball cap that bore the logo of Michigan State University and was dressed in a blue sweater and blue jeans. I walked up to the table. She looked up at me as she sipped her coffee.

"Something I can do for you?" she asked with a wry smile.

"I'm Miller Rixey. I am pretty sure I was supposed to meet you."

Her laughter was melodic, "I know who you are. I was just messing with you. I spotted you the moment you walked in. I was wondering how long it would take you to find me. Please sit, I'm sure you're hungry. I know I never eat much on long flights."

"Thanks," I said as I took a seat.

I picked up a four-language menu and had made my decision as the waitress appeared. I pointed at what I wanted and nodded my head when she held the coffee pot. She took my order and left.

"Sorry you didn't pay attention in Spanish class in high school?" she scolded.

I sheepishly nodded.

She leaned over to the table and passed me a gold wedding band. "Put this on and never take it off. It has a tracking device. So. if you ever get lost or otherwise vanish, I will be able to find you. She held up her hand showing an engagement ring and a wedding ring on it. Besides, we are supposed to be married as cover for your assignment."

I slipped the ring on and sat there looking at her.

Her tone changed to one of concern, "How's Gramps doing? I know he tried to keep what happened to him from me."

I laughed, "Willard is doing fine. He's a tough guy to keep down. I expect him out of the hospital shortly. He sends his best."

Morgan nodded, "Thanks and thank you for taking care of the man that did that to him."

I looked somewhat surprised that she knew about what happened.

"I hear things. You saved me from hunting the person down myself."

Just then the waitress returned with my order, refilled our coffee and left.

"So, who were those other assholes that were with Herr Steele that I saw you talking to?"

"You know Steele?"

She nodded, "Yes. I've actually been down here for the past three months. He has something to do with some right-wing paramilitary outfit. He is very dangerous. I don't know who the other two are." She shrugged, "Probably local muscle. His group, Eva Perón *Frente de Liberación* (EPFL), are suspected in a series of bombings and other terrorist attacks. We don't know if this is going to lead to something bigger, like a coup or what."

I nodded, "Yes, most former STASI Colonels have that reputation. Willard sent me a message informing me of that fact. I have met him twice now and don't look forward to another meeting."

Morgan looked surprised, "We hadn't heard that part of his biography, that may come in handy at some point."

We sat in silence as the waitress cleared our dishes and refilled our coffee.

"You know why I am here?"

"Yes, some artifact that our government wants to get their hands on. Caesar's Medallion I believe it's called. Bobby seems to think there is some connection between the Medallion and Adolf Hitler. I find the whole story simply too hard to believe. I mean didn't he die in 1945?"

"Nope. That's what the conspirators would want you to think. Based on the information that friends of Willard had sent him." I went on to explain in detail all I had read and what conclusions I had come to. "Basically, Hitler had indeed escaped Germany with the assistance of our government. I was positive Hitler was dead. I was just as positive that Caesar's Medallion was involved in some sort of strange conspiracy," I sat back when I was finished.

Morgan looked aghast, "On the surface, based on the attacks and your contacts with Herr Steele, what you say makes sense." She shrugged, "I now see why Gramps turned his agency over to you," she added with a smile. She shifted in her seat, "You must be exhausted from that trip. I know I am after a long flight. I have us checked in at a very nice hotel. After you get cleaned up and get some sleep, we can discuss our plans for tomorrow. I assume you will be wanting to visit La Recoleta Cemetery to check out the Eva Peron connection? She slowly stood. She still looked like she knew her way around the courts. I was guessing she hadn't gained five pounds since college.

I stood up and picked up both our bills, "Wouldn't miss it for the world." I grabbed my bag and paid our bill and we left the diner.

We left the relative comfort of the terminal. We stepped outside and to heard a car engine racing and wheels squealing. A flurry of automatic weapons fire erupted. I saw Morgan react like she had been struck by a lightning bolt. Her body twisted as she did a header into the glass door and then slumped to the ground. I ran to where she laid, along with about a dozen other people all either dead or critically wounded.

The scene was total chaos. The shrill howl of police and ambulance alarms filled the air. People were screaming and begging for help. The smell of gunpowder hung in the air. It required all of my training and discipline that I could muster to focus on my immediate problem at hand, Morgan. Christ, how could this happen I wondered? I was pretty sure that attack and been meant for me. I knelt down beside her. I rolled her over and found three bullet holes in her sweater. She was breathing but unconscious. That was at least, a good start.

Chapter Sixteen

"Death is nothing, but to live defeated and inglorious is to die daily."
Napoleon Bonaparte

I couldn't believe there was no blood either leaking from Morgan or no traces of blood on her. After all, I knew at a minimum of three rounds had entered her. The lack of blood gave me hope as I lifted her sweater, she was a real pro, she had been wearing a vest. I was able to pull the three rounds out of her and quickly placed them in my pocket. It looked like she was going to end up with a black eye from her header into the door, but nothing life-threatening. I looked out of the corner of my eye and saw the Major I had dealt with earlier, followed by ten of his men, sprinting toward the door with their weapons drawn. They were going to be a day late and a dollar short. However, I didn't want to be around to answer any questions. I knew my diplomatic passport would mean I didn't have to say anything, but they could put me on the next flight back to the USA. First major assignment ending in failure. No way! I struggled to get Morgan to her feet.

"Come on Morgan, upsy daisy. Walkies. We got to get the hell out of here." I looked back at the Major and his crew, they would be at the entrance to the terminal momentarily.

She groaned, but with my aid, we were able to get her moving.

"Where's your car?"

"Took a cab."

I guided us down toward the cab.

"We got a safe house or some such thing?"

She gasped and grabbed her ribs, "Hotel."

We made it to a cab that was just outside the range of view of the shootings. The Major and his group exploded out the doorway. It looked like they would have plenty to do besides looking for people who had fled the scene. I pushed Morgan into the cab and told her to tell the driver where we were going.

For my part, I kept looking through the rear window and only finally relaxing as the airport shooting scene slowly drifted out of sight. I turned around and let out a brief sigh.

I heard a brief exchange between Morgan and the dr iver in Spanish and almost before I could close the door, the cab had hurtled away from the curb. I saw Morgan holding her side and heard her groan again as I saw her reach for her pocket.

"What's wrong? We got to get you to a hospital."

"No hospital," she wheezed, "the hotel."

She gasped again, "My fucking ribs feel like they were cracked, I am hoping they are only bruised. Reach into my pocket and pull out my cash."

I pulled her cash out, "Now what?"

She sat up a little straighter, "Peel off the four top bills for the driver. If you got it, add another two hundred American and give it back to me."

I handed her a mixed pile of cash. She smiled, "Now as long as there or no sudden movements or stretching, I will be good till we get back to the room."

The driver, an older man, was totally bald, and clean shaven. Beyond that, who knew.

Morgan spoke to him in Spanish and the driver blanched. To his credit though, he never took his eyes off the streets and the traffic. He was a true master of the streets as he expertly navigated the traffic, driving at breakneck speed. This guy had clearly missed his calling, I am sure he could put many racecar drivers to shame. The cab came to a lurch in front of our hotel. Morgan swore and grabbed her side. I heard her gasp for breath. This time I didn't require a translator as she said some words that would make the most hardened sailor blush.

She spoke to the man again, this time his color returned, and he broke into a smile. The only thing I understood in the entire conversatio n was when the driver said, *Sí. Gracias. Estaré disponible para su jefe."*

The doorman was decked out in an ornate uniform, complete with cap and epaulets on his shoulders. He looked to be a swarthy fellow, probably a few years younger than me. He reached for the door handle and pulled it open, "Glad to see you again, *Señora* Rixey" as he held his hand out to help her out of the car. He turned to me, "Nice to meet you, Señor Rixey. May I help you with your bag?"

"No thanks." I took Morgan's roll out of my pocket and hoped I guessed right when I peeled off a denomination with a ten on it. I handed it to him and he smiled and nodded. Morgan had seen the entire transaction and winked at me.

The doorman led us up to the stairs to the hotel lobby, opened the door, and after we entered let it close and then resumed his position behind a desk.

"What the hell did you say to that cabby?"

"I told him we worked for one of the cartels and we knew who he was and he did not know who we worked for. When I handed him the money, I asked him for his phone number and told him we might require his services."

"I caught what he said to you, in this macho country it's quite an accomplishment to have a man call a woman boss." I grinned, well at least we made it here, I was having some doubts."

She nodded, "I can have that effect on people when I choose to."

We shortly arrived at the front desk. The attendant wore a nametag that identified her a Maria S. She looked to be about as tall as Morgan, but much, much thinner. She was a brunette. She was fashionably outfitted in a very sharp looking blue blazer and skirt. She seemed like someone who genuinely enjoyed helping her customers.

"Any messages for Room 237?" Morgan asked.

"No Ma'am." She turned to face me. "And you must be Señor Rixey? Your wife said you were arriving on a later flight and what a wonderful person you were."

"Did she?" I smiled. "That was nice of you, dear."

Looking very serious the clerk said, "Oh yes sir. My name is Maria and I will be here until seven this morning. If you have any questions or need anything, please don't hesitate to call."

Morgan squeezed my arm and caused it to go numb, "Coming, dear? We don't want to keep poor Maria from her work," she said between gritted teeth. Morgan smiled at Maria," Thank you, young lady."

Holding onto my arm, she guided me to the elevator. With the grip, she had on my arm, I really had no choice but to follow. My arm felt it was on fire. I tried to free it, but she had a firm grip on the situation, mainly my arm.

"Two things, one that hurts, so ease up." I felt her relax her hold, "Oh I didn't want you spending all night commiserating with Maria, Morgan said with an evil grin. I rubbed my arm bringing back the feeling in it.

"What's the second thing?" Morgan asked, in a voice dripping in ice.

Working my fingers to get the blood flowing in them, I asked, "You ever see The Shining?"

"I have. I had to suffer through it in a films class while attending college."

"Then you might understand why I get nervous about Room 237."

She laughed and then groaned, clutching her ribs, "You are going to have to tough it out, Miller."

I pushed a button calling a car down to us. When we got in, I saw Morgan push the two button and we rode up in silence. We were treated to a brief exposure to Herb Alpert's rendition of Spanish Flea. There was a ding as the elevator announced our arrival on the second floor. There was a brief pause and then the door opened.

Morgan and I stepped into a richly furnished corridor. Fine oil paintings hung on the walls; the carpet was a red velour that felt quite thick. Some of the windows were open and the now heavy rain began blowing in. I even noticed some potted plants spread out about every twenty feet apart. I grinned to myself, this isn't the Motel Six, is it?

Morgan said, "Two doors down on our left." She stopped and reached into her purse. She pulled out a small brown wooden box and handed it to me. She looked sheepishly," Meant to give this to you back at the airport." She shrugged, "Shall we say things got a little confused?"

I opened the box and nodded. There was a Glock-17, a fully loaded magazine and a suppressor in the box. I handed her back the box. I checked the magazine and nodded approvingly; it had been loaded the way I liked it. I slid it into the handle and then screwed the suppressor on and pulled back on the slide to put a round in the chamber. For the first time since St. Louis, I felt safe. I slid the pistol in my jacket pocket.

"There are three more loaded magazines and two boxes of 9MM ammunition in the room safe. I hope this more than suffices for this case," she said handing me the key card.

As I bent over to slide the card key into the slot, I could hear the sound of footsteps seemed to be running away from the door. I saw Morgan draw her pistol at the same time I did, and I pushed the door open. The light indicator went from blank to green signifying successful entry.

I saw a figure dressed from head to toe in black dive looking like he was getting ready to dive off our balcony. I fired three rounds and was pretty sure I'd missed with all three. I swore to myself as I ran to the balcony area. What the hell was happening here?

Chapter Seventeen

"Don't become a mere recorder of facts, but try to penetrate the mystery of their origin." Ivan Pavlov

Like a fool, I charged onto the balcony forgetting one important rule; it's not a smart idea run on surfaces that are wet and smooth. I lost my footing and was out of control. I flung my arms wildly in a futile attempt to regain my traction.

When I saw that it looked like I was going to go flying over the edge of the balcony, I had the presence of mind to begin a slide that would have made any NFL Quarterback proud. I slid into the wall on the terrace, with little hurt except maybe my pride.

Morgan had made it out to the balcony as I hit the wall. "You okay," she asked?" the apprehension clearly in her voice.

We both looked over the ledge and saw about thirty feet down saw what looked like a small trampoline type pad. As we didn't see any bodies lying on the ground, we had to assume the figure had escaped. The storm seemed to be coming down heavier and heavier. As we started to go back inside, Morgan pointed excitedly.

"Look."

I looked and saw a pool of blood. "Wow, I did hit him and looks like he's hurt bad." We stepped inside and closed the sliding glass door. "We need to check and see if our visitor left us any presents behind."

Morgan nodded, "Take a seat if you please, I can do this much quicker alone, then with both of us checking." She pulled a wand similar, though smaller than the one I use in my office. She extended it and turned it on and began walking in our living room area. No beeps heard. She then went into my bedroom. I lost track of what she was doing.

I picked up the TV remote and hit power. I began surfing channels until I found a news channel that spoke English. It happened to be one of the major American news networks international division. The lead and currently only story was the attack Morgan and I had survived at the airport. I heard the sirens of ambulances and police cars in the background of the live report. I hit the mute button so as not disturb Morgan as she searched for whatever our uninvited guest had left us. I watched for a few more minutes and looked up when I heard Morgan come out of her bedroom. She had her right hand full of something.

I looked up, "Find anything of interest?"

Wordlessly, she sat down next to me and laid a half dozen two inch by one-inch white squares on the table. They had a black wire running out one side and a multicolored wire, which I guessed was the transmitter.

I looked at her quizzically.

Morgan reported, "These are Bodil eavesdropping devices. Made in East Germany back in the 1980s. They were the preferred bug of STASI. Do we know of anyone involved in this case who was involved with STASI?"

I rolled my eyes, "Yes, we sure do." I chuckled, "So did they teach you about East German espionage gear in Protocol Officers School or perhaps while you were in the Amy."

"Not exactly," she replied in a tone that meant that discussion was over.

"Oh yes, I found these slugs in your vest." I reached into my pocket and laid them out on the table."

Morgan looked at the slugs; they were all severely flattened. "I'm sure could identify these if we had the proper equipment, but we don't. I'm not sure what good it would do to be able to identify them anyway. I'm under orders to approach the American Embassy only in matters of life and death. Sorry to say, this isn't one of them." She shrugged, "I'll hang on to them but don't get your hopes up."

I turned my attention back to the TV and clicked off the mute button. "... Al Qaeda and the notorious right-wing group, Eva Perón Frente de Liberación have taken joint credit for the attack on the airport terminal today that so far has killed twenty-two..." I put the TV back on mute. If this were like most stories of its type, it would be running for days.

"Did you check and make sure they hadn't messed with your laptop?"

Morgan nodded, "It was off and locked in the room safe. Just a habit I got into. To get into the safe without my knowledge required them to crack a six-number code and not disturb a hair I had left on the top and bottom of the safe door. I checked it anyway, it was fine."

Good. We can talk later, but I know you want to want to hit the shower and examine those ribs and I need one after my long flight. An hour later, we were both back on the couch watching the news, clad in our fluffy hotel robes. Morgan had popped two pills and sighed contently as she had an ice bag on her ribs.

"How are you feeling, Morgan?"

"This wasn't as bad as either of us thought at first. I'll be fine. I would get hurt worse than this when I played basketball. Ice and some pain relievers and I will be good."

Morgan had already fallen asleep on the couch; I was still glued to the TV. A loud pounding on the door caught my attention and woke up Morgan. She slowly got to her feet. I motioned her back down.

"Hotel Security, Mr. Rixey, came through the door in perfect, and an unaccented English.

"Give me a moment, I need to put on my robe." I quickly called down to the front desk. The phone was answered on the first ring. "Maria, do you know who this is?"

"Oh yes, Señor Rixey. How can I be of assistance to you?"

"Do you know any reason your Hotel Security team would be knocking on my door at this hour?"

"Mr. Rixey, we do not have a Hotel Security Team."

"Then call the police quickly and tell them we have two criminal types beating on our door, trying to get in." I hung up the phone, not even bothering to wait for a response.

"We are in some deep shit, Maria said there was no security team for this hotel. Coppers on the way At least I hope so. We need to stall for as much time as we can," I rasped.

Morgan nodded acknowledgment. She had her weapon drawn as did I. We stood to the side of the door. I motioned for her to drop down to one knee. She nodded and quickly did.

"Mr. Rixey, please come to the door now. It is most important that we speak to immediately. If you do not come to the door at once, we will be forced to get the police involved. You most certainly do not want that."

Stalling for time, and never intending to step in front of the door anyway, I asked, "Can you hold your ID to the eyehole? I need to see it. You know what they say in hotels when it comes to guest security."

The response was four bullets through the door. I watched in amazement as the door seemed to disintegrate before my eyes. I heard screaming and more shooting in the hallway followed by a couple of loud thuds. Another knock on the door.

Chapter Eighteen

"Never was anything great achieved without danger."
Niccolo Machiavelli

Warily keeping my distance from the door, I replied back, "Who is it?"

"Buenos Aires Police, please open the door."

I looked at Morgan and she nodded. I handed her my pistol and headed for the door. The accent sounded right, unlike the obvious Americans who had been at our door moments earlier. I opened the door and viewed the chaos that was occurring in the corridor. People were screaming and yelling. I saw four men loading up the two bodies in body bags. I saw the man in my doorway barking orders and gradually the bodies were removed and calm had been restored. He answered his cell phone and talked briefly. He became slightly animated during the discussion. I could not imagine he was having a very good day between the airport shooting and here.

The man now turned his attention to me. He was a heavyset man, around my height, jet black hair, and wore a lanyard with a gold badge around his neck. I could sense this was not a man to be taken lightly, his aura radiated power and authority.

"I am Chief Inspector Carlos Gomez of the Special Investigation Division of the Buenos Aires Police. You would be Señor Miller Rixey?"

"Yes, sir."

"Do you have any explanation as to why those two men would be attempting to get into your room? This incident as you can see has caused a great deal of disruption." He looked at me with a very grim expression on his face.

I had a pretty good idea why they had been trying to break in, but much like my interview with the U.S. Attorney back in St. Louis, this was not the time or place to be advancing theories, I shrugged, "Maybe a group that was targeting tourists?" I really have no idea."

He smirked, "Señor, we will accept that explanation for now, out of respect for your diplomatic status."

I tried to hide my surprise at that last statement but apparently did not do a very good job of it.

"Don't look so surprised Señor, we know you and the lovely Señora Rixey both carry diplomatic passports from the United States. You are not suspected of committing any crimes in Argentina, so if you say you don 't know what happened."

Morgan stepped to the door, "Did I hear my name being mentioned?"

The Inspector actually cracked a smile and bowed, "So very nice to meet you, Señora. I only wish it was under better circumstances. It was most fortunate that we were able to locate you. I am so glad neither of you was hurt. We had your pictures on various airport security cameras a nd we knew you had been at the airport at the time of the shooting. We wanted to question you briefly about that."

"I understand completely Inspector, to say the least, the situation was extremely terrifying. I was fortunate enough to stumble when the shooting began and was spared. Miller picked me up and we made it to a cab. Other than that, I don't think I can add anything to help you. I will certainly not let this unsettling experience influence how I feel about your lovely country. We had planned to contact the police, but you understand how things are, don't you Inspector?" Morgan said with an absolutely straight face.

The Inspector nodded, "Your purpose for coming here was listed as tourism?"

"Yes sir, we plan to see some sites while we are down here."

"Very well, I know I will have more questions for the both of you about this incident and the airport shooting. For now, my number one priority is the airport shooting. I will be assigning a group of men to investigate your incident." He smiled at Morgan and bowed again, kissing her hand when she offered it. All I got was the perfunctory handshake.

I stepped into the corridor and all was now quiet, I saw Inspector Carlos quietly talking with the few of his remaining men. The elevator dinged, signaling its arrival on our floor and the door slowly opened.

Maria from the front desk approached us. She was followed by three staff members, "Señor and Señora, I am very sorry for what has happened here. We will move you to a new room." She looked askance at the door and shook her head. She handed me the card key for room 796. "George Kaplan's room in North by Northwest, I thought instinctively.

"Thank you, Maria. We realize this wasn't your fault. If you can give us a few minutes to get our things from the room safe, we will let your staff do the moving. You were a real lifesaver. Who knows what those men had planned for us? Thank you so much," Morgan said with a warm smile.

Maria nodded, "Now I have other guests to hand hold with, enjoy the rest of the evening the best you can."

About twenty minutes later we were safely ensconced in Room 796. I collapsed on the couch and turned the TV on. I found the channel I was looking for. The story was the same; it was continuing coverage of the "Airport Massacre" as it was now being called. The death toll was now at thirty and expected to rise. Morgan had taken her wand out and began checking the rooms. I paid close attention to the replays of the films to see if Morgan and I showed up in any of them.

Morgan came back into the living room, smiling, "All clear here. The room safe combination is 1776."

I motioned for her to join me on the couch, "Look, we both know at a minimum I was the main target for the drive by. You and the others were all collateral damage. These people, whoever they are very determined that I not find the Medallion." I counted off on my fingers, "We have the two visits from Herr Steele, the drive-by shooting, the room is bugged, the break into our room, and finally the two American thugs who tried to get in our door. This case has gotten far more dangerous than I thought it would be."

Morgan nodded, "It's pretty clear someone thinks you know more than you do and now you pose a threat to the people who control the Medallion. Two things, then I have to go to bed. First, we will need to be on our toes later tonight when we visit the cemetery and second, I will root around and see if I can find out who those two Americans were that tried to break into our room. She shrugged, "Good night, Miller, "she said sweetly.

I headed to my bedroom, set up my computer, and then laid down on my bed to rest my eyes. I looked at my watch and saw it was 4:30 AM. I woke with a start a few minutes later and looked at my watch again, it was now 3:30 PM. I checked my emails, forwarding what was relevant to Ms. Nickels and then turned my laptop off. I headed to the restroom and a half an hour later, I was ready to face the world. I quickly dressed only pausing to put on a shoulder holster. I slid my pistol, the suppressor still connected into the holster. After what had happened last night, I was not going to go around this town unarmed. I pulled my bomber jacket on and grabbed my fedora.

I went to knock on Morgan's door and saw a note thumbtacked to it: "Miller, hopefully, I will be back by the time you wake up. I will be hanging out in the hotel lounge. See you then. M"

As I walked down the corridor to the elevator, I was glad to see there were no signs of what had happened last night. The hotel must have a pretty efficient cleaning crew, I couldn't even see a bloodstain on the carpet, I thought. Before I got in the elevator, I doublechecked to make sure my phone was in my jacket pocket. I then press the down key. I got in and rode it down, enjoying the musical strains of the theme to The Third Man. The elevator landed with a lurch and the door opened. I saw one of the two bodyguards I had met earlier in the morning that had been with Herr Steele. He approached me in the menacing way only bullies and thugs seem to be able to. I reached into my jacket pocket and pressed the button that activated the two thongs on my phone that served as a TASER. He stopped for a moment in an attempt to size me up. I could see a look of concern flicker across his face. This guy was pretty good. He quickly regained his composure.

"Herr Steele wishes to see you at once in the hotel lounge," he said with a strong German accent. It was a tone of voice that told me he would not take no for an answer.

"Oh, it speaks. Please tell your master if he wishes to speak to me, he may call and make an appointment." I paused to let that sink in. "By the way, what happened to your boyfriend?" As I spoke, I quickly checked the lobby, I was very much alone.

The bodyguard moved closer and smiled ruthlessly, "Nein, Herr Rixey, you will come with me now. I will search you. Herr Steele requires it."

"Not a chance, Fritz. I won't stand for a frisk from the likes of you. You understand that?"

The bodyguard smiled and licked his lips, "I was hoping you would say that. I am going to enjoy this." He closed to arm's length away from me.

I knew this guy would kick my ass in a fair fight, so time to be unfair. I jabbed the tongs from the phone in his neck and pressed the button again. I saw his eyes roll to the back of his head and saw his body jump around like one might see a puppet in a puppet show. I made a mental note to write the manufacturer and tell them how well their item worked. I'd have time for that later. I quickly checked the lobby; it was empty except for some people near the desk. We hadn't been seen. I promptly searched him and relieved him of his small-bore pistol.

As he started to come back to his senses, I grabbed him and said, "This will really put you in tight with your boss. Now let's go see him." I twisted one of his arms behind his back and began to frog march him toward the lounge. He tried to protest and I slapped him. He complained more and my response was to twist his arm harder. He had been caught by surprise and totally lost his composure. He was, from the tone of his voice, cursing me in German. He had underestimated me once; I knew he wouldn't make that mistake again.

I entered the lounge; it was dark and cool. I saw Morgan sitting at the bar, drinking something. My timing couldn't have been better. I didn't want to draw any more attention to myself than I already had. Only Morgan and Herr Steele were in the lounge. She at first looked at me somewhat confused. Then once she realized what had happened, she broke into a grin.

I walked to the table that Herr Steele was seated at. I tossed the weapon that I had taken from the bodyguard on the table. It hit with a clatter and then slid off and rested by Herr Steele's feet. I gave the bodyguard a shove into the wall next to the Steele's table. He crashed against the wall with a most satisfactory thud. I could tell Steele was not amused.

"Some friendly advice, you shouldn't give weapons to people who don't know what they are doing with them. They might hurt themselves. Luckily for your bodyguard, I stepped in right after I saw a ten-year-old disarm him."

Steele said something in German to the bodyguard. I was pretty sure he wasn't telling him about what a great job he had done bringing me here. The bodyguard glowered as he went to another table and sat down. He continued to stare at me angrily. I knew I had made a friend for life.

"Unless you want another lesson, mind your manners. It isn't polite to stare," I warned him.

I sat down at the table, ordered a drink from the waiter. I kept my eyes on Herr Steele. I knew the goon would not do anything unless Steele ordered it. I fumbled in my pockets and could not find any of my cigars. I did have a crumpled pack of Lucky Strikes. I pulled one out and lit it. "Now Herr Steele, you got me here. What was so important?"

Chapter Nineteen

"I have always thought the actions of men the best interpreters of their thoughts." John Locke

The bartender arrived with my drink. I thanked him and nodded in Morgan's direction and told him to put it on her tab, He nodded and walked away. I was not about to give Herr Steele my room number that easily. Make the bastard work for it, I thought.

I blew smoke in Herr Steele's face. He coughed and made one of those pitiful waving motions that people believe will clear the air of all pollution. "Herr Rixey, perhaps we have misjudged you. All we knew about you as you were very inexperienced in handling cases of this nature and you had a natural affinity for, um shall we say, looking the other way or burying evidence when it financially suited you. We know your mentor, Mr. Bishop did all the heavy lifting in your agency," he said in a raspy tone of voice.

I shrugged. I knew this was an immature attempt to bait me, I was not going to allow that to work. "I guess you can write this off as beginner's luck on my part. As for the crooked part, don't be too sure I am as crooked as people would tell you. Having a reputation like that is good for bringing in the really tough cases and gives me access to places and people that the good guys never see or make it to."

Steele pondered what I had said. While he sat there, I said, "Anyway, Her Steele, you went through a great deal of effort to get me here. Was it simply to talk about my shortcomings? If so, I think you covered them adequately. I really need to be going, I am planning on having a wonderful dinner at one of your best restaurants," I rose to my feet and began to walk away from the table.

He raised his bony hand, "Please Herr Rixey, don't be so impatient. I just want to talk to you. Perhaps allay your fears and concerns about specific topics. You do like talking, don't you?

"I love talking as long as the topic or the person interests me."

Steele seemed delighted. I actually saw him break into a smile. He leaned over the table, "Very good. I don't like dealing with people who don't like to talk. I view them as unreliable. I mean being good at anything requires practice, doesn't it? If you are closed-lipped, then you cannot ever be good at talking?"

I looked confused for a moment as I attempted to untangle precisely what the hell he had just said. I knew he had gotten plenty of people to talk during his career with the STASI. I knew him to be the type of man who never said or did anything without good reason. More than one person has lost their life by underestimating their opponent. I was not about to join that class.

"Fair enough. I have a subject I would love to talk about. Can we talk about Caesar's Medallion?"

Herr Steele coolly nodded. He was every bit the professional I feared he was. I had rattled him at the airport, but I could see that it was not going to happen again. He slid me two envelopes, one very thick and one very thin. "You will find traveling money in one envelope and in the other, research that proves the fact that Caesar's Medallion was taken by the Russians in 1945. They discovered it when they searched Herr Hitler's desk, it is currently being held by the FSB. Please examine the documentation at your leisure, and I wish you the best of luck in Russia. In the meantime, enjoy yourself for a few days."

"Thank you, Herr Steele. If what you say is true, we will see the sights for a few days, consult with my client, and probably be on our way to Russia."

I stood up and offered my hand, we shook, his hand was cold and clammy. The fact that he shook hands with me made me think he had convinced me about Russia. I took this as a tell that he was lying and the documentation was made and he was lying through his yellow stained teeth.

I waited for him and his bodyguard to leave and then I joined Morgan at the bar.

I motioned to the bartender and signaled for refills of what had been drinking. I took out another cigarette and lit it. I inhaled deeply, enjoying the burn. I turned to Morgan, "Did you find anything out about the two men from last night?"

Morgan thanked the bartender for the refill and waited until he left. "Yes, the two men who tried to get in our room were dead. They had died three years ago, in a helicopter crash in Afghanistan."

I groaned inwardly, "I never told you because quite frankly I didn't think it was important, the man who attacked your grandfather had also died in a helicopter accident in Afghanistan."

I looked up at the ceiling of the lounge, thinking and hoping the answer would be there, it finally registered, "June 6,2013."

"My, how odd. You will never guess the day they supposedly died?"

"Don't tell me, let me guess. June 6, 2013?"

"Wow, smart as well as handsome," Morgan said with a wry smile.

I nodded and had a good laugh myself.

"Did you happen to catch the unit? I'm not sure that matters Three dead the same day from a helicopter accident? Go figure."

I shook my head no, "It was a pretty short and to the point report. The report said he was Special Forces and that most of his duty assignments had been redacted." I pulled another cigarette out of its pack and lit it. "Listen, I knew there was a level of danger with this case when I took it. It has gotten much worse than I had bargained for. We got crazed locals, Nazis, former STATSI members, American mercenaries, and a good chance that ODESSA its self who seem to want us not to be able to find the Medallion. What do you think? I mean Herr Steele gave me travel money and documentation that is supposed to show that the Medallion is in Russia. I'm thinking Russia is looking much safer and much nicer than here."

Morgan huffed, "Miller John Rixey, you cannot be serious."

I smiled and winced at hearing my middle name. My mom had been the only one to address me that way and usually meant I was in big trouble. The bartender came back to where Morgan and I had been sitting.

"Everything okay here?"

Morgan smiled sweetly, "Everything is fine. Thank you."

I shook my head, "I was just trying to inject a little gallows humor into this crummy situation. Keep in mind that Russia is very nice this time of year."

She scowled. I could tell she was not impressed by my miserable attempt at being witty. She held out her hand.

Morgan said, "Hand me that envelope that is supposed to have the documentation about the Medallion." I handed it to her. She opened the envelope. She read through the five-page report rather quickly, folded it up, and handed it back to me. "My Russian is a little rusty and the report looks like it could be legitimate; I mean the right seals are in the right places and the report makes sense..."

"But?"

Morgan thought for a moment, "There are some problems with the way the report feels."

"Feels?" I asked wishing she would stop talking in riddles.

"I mean I know this is a copy of a report, so that would explain why the seals aren't raised and would also explain the lack of indentations on the paper." She paused again, "I can tell you with one hundred percent certainty that this report was not typed on the day it says on the report."

"You're killing me, Morgan, how do you know this stuff?" The bartender checked back and I asked for two cups of coffee with plenty of cream and sugar. Drinking time was over.

"First of all, the lines are too perfectly spaced and everything is too neatly done. You ever use a regular typewriter?"

"A few times."

"Did anything ever line up exactly? I mean you had some up and down lines, right? And that reason was you weren't a professional secretary. I doubt if they would have let a secretary near this report. Probably would have been typed by an agent or perhaps a cipher clerk."

She paused as the bartender returned with our coffee. When he left to tend to other customers, she continued.

"Finally, this is the totally wrong font type. Yes, it's written in Cyrillic, but I have seen Russian documents from that era, this isn't real.

Someone, no doubt used a version of a word processor that was able to type in Russian. Not a bad job. Their bad luck you were working with me."

"That sounds solid to me. I didn't trust Steele to begin with. I was wondering what his end game was. I mean giving me a lot of cash and documentation to prove where the Medallion was. It doesn't make sense." I looked at my watch. "We have a little trip we need to get prepared for. It will be dark soon."

We got up, I left a generous tip for the bartender and we headed to the elevator bank and back up to our room. Some preparations were required for our journey to the Cemetery.

Chapter Twenty

"In looking back, I see nothing to regret and little to correct."
John C. Calhoun

As we rode the elevator back down to the lobby, Morgan took my arm and cooed, "Miller, I am really struggling to figure you out. I know you're smart, Gramps wouldn't have turned the firm over to a dullard. You seem so unassuming, but you sure can handle yourself. What say when this case is solved, we get to know each other better?"

Her grasp on my arm was pleasant, not like the one that blocked nerve endings. I smiled, "Well Morgan, I am trying to figure out whether you bailed on the Army or the Army bailed on you. Your knowledge about certain topics and the way you appear to be able to handle yourself impresses me. It's a date. The best hotel in DC?"

She gave me a quick hug and a peck on the cheek.

"Sounds great. That's contingent on you being able to take some time off from your duties as a Protocol Officer in London."

She giggled, "I think I can swing some either vacation days or sick days off. I guess the embassy will have to learn to do without me for a few weeks, maybe? I have every confidence they will survive without my helping hands."

I got one question, Miller, "How did you handle that big guy who was with Steele? He had you by fifty pounds and maybe 15 years."

I grinned, "I cannot tell a lie. I used a TASER on him." I pulled out my phone from my jacket pocket and showed her how it worked. I could tell she was impressed.

"You should have seen the look on Steele's face when you brought that young idiot in. I thought he was going to have a stroke."

I nodded. We rode the rest of the way in silence. The bell rang announcing our arrival on the lobby floor, the door opened, and we stepped out.

We walked through a fairly crowded, well-lit lobby. I saw Maria working at the front desk. I turned to a TV monitor and saw there was still wall to wall coverage of the Airport Shootings. I checked out the people in the lobby. If there was someone who was planning to follow us, I couldn't tell. I was hoping the bad weather might discourage people from following. Not likely, but you never know. The weather looked particularly nasty outside. The same doorman who was working last night was on duty again. He opened the door for us.

"Get you two a cab?"

Morgan shook her head, "No thank you."

"Kind of nasty weather for a walk. You two have a good evening. If you decide to catch a cab on the way back, please call the hotel and we will send someone for you."

Once we cleared the overhang of the hotel, it felt like we had entered an alien world. The cool, dry, and well-lit world of the hotel lobby and been replaced by one where the cold rain continued to cascade down on the street, the streetlights seemed to be fighting a losing struggle with the darkness, and a thick fog had rolled in that limited vision of those on the streets. Even the shadows seemed much too black. When the wind would occasionally gust, driving the rain harder, it would stir the trees that lined the streets, and their shadows would change in a disquieting way. I had never seen a situation before and hopefully would never see such a situation again. It was a perfect storm of the elements.

As we walked to the La Recoleta Cemetery, I thought I heard footsteps behind us. I would stop and turn and see nothing but the barely visible flickering street lamps. Despite what my eyes didn't see, I was confident we were being followed.

"What's wrong, Miller? "Morgan asked with apprehension in her voice. I could feel her body trembling as she spoke.

"I can't be sure. I have the feeling we are being followed. I think I am hearing footsteps, but of that, I can't be sure. When I turn around, I don't see anyone. I've been doing this type of work for a long time and I am tough to follow. I don't know..., "my voice trailing off as I shrugged my shoulders.

Morgan spoke softly, "This whole scene of going to the Cemetery late at night and the weather would put anyone on edge. I don't ever recall being out on a stranger feeling evening before, including my time in Afghanistan." She added with a soft and reassuring tone, "I had been out in the field on some very terrifying nights there, but nothing like this. Trust your training and your instincts, I know that's what I do." She squeezed my arm reassuringly.

I nodded and we moved on. No one with any sense was out in this weather. We hadn't seen anyone since leaving the safe confines of the hotel and had only seen maybe a half dozen vehicles on the streets.

We shortly arrived at our destination. A sign on the heavy metal front door proclaimed: La Recoleta Cemetery. In English and Spanish, right below the name were the listed hours. Naturally, we were after hours. That was to be expected. We received our first bit of bad news. Someone had forced the gate open. I took out my flashlight and worked it around the outside of the cemetery. The power of the concentrated beam of six thousand lumens cut through the inky blackness like a knife. I saw the cemetery itself was additionally protected by high stone walls. It was built like a fort. The owners of this place were serious about keeping people out after hours. We really had no other choice but to enter through the already forced open door. I gently pushed the unprotected gate open. It made a slight squeak, but to me, it seemed as loud as an explosion. I could hear voices of various accents, German, Spanish, and American. I turned to Morgan, she has just finished screwing her suppressor in place and was reaching for a flashlight similar to mine.

We were about twenty feet inside the cemetery when I heard a voice came out of the darkness, "Herr Rixey and Fräulein Blake it is, how we say, most unfortunate that you chose to ignore my generous offer." We slowly turned around to face Steele. "You will do well to put your hands up. You have my promise I will make what will happen to you as painless as possible. You both will soon be dead and nothing will be able to stop us."

I looked at Morgan and she had already dropped her gun and had her arms raised. I knew it was certain death to try to get into an active shootout with an unknown and armed group of people. The minions of Herr Steele rapidly closed in to take us prisoner. This had all the makings of a very bad day.

Chapter Twenty-one

"That which does not kill us makes us stronger." Friedrich Nietzsche

I have had my fair share of what I considered to be low points during my thirty-seven years on this planet. It's all part of life. Sometimes good things happen; sometimes bad things happen. I can safely say that this was easily the worst of my low points. I was sure Morgan had a similar feeling. It seemed like they had a chance to kill us before we would even realize what happened. I realized that a shootout against an unknown number of bad guys, that we couldn't even see was not the way to do things. Some minions of Herr Steele appeared like phantoms out of the darkness. They were clad in black outfits and all wore black ski masks.

One of the minions stepped forward toward me and removed his mask. It was the guy I called Fritz who I had taken in the hotel. Two of the minions approached Morgan, one grabbed her arm and twisted it behind her back. The other one began fondling her.

"I wouldn't do that," she warned.

"Shut up bitch, I will do want I want with you. What are you going to do about it?" the minion in front of her taunted.

Fritz sensing the situation was well in hand turned his attention to me, "Herr Rixey, my brother died from the gunshot wounds you inflicted on him. You humiliated me. Before I am done with you, you will be begging me to kill you," he screamed as his voice echoed off the various monuments. He pulled a very long and I was sure a very sharp knife from a belt. He closed in on me. I knew I had to do something.

As the man stepped in to carry out his threat, my heart pounded wildly. I knew I had to do something to something and fast. I took a step backward and lowered myself into a crouch to prepare myself for the attack. My fear soon turned to amusement. I saw he had a dancing red dot on his forehead. Somewhere in the darkness, someone had our back. I couldn't help but smile. Steele screamed something to him in German, but my attacker couldn't hear him. He had tunnel vision and was focused on me. Neither the warning nor the dot on his head c ould keep him from his mission.

Without a sound, the top of my tormentor's head disintegrated. The force of the shot forced him backward, I heard the knife clatter as it fell from his hand and watched as he dropped in slow motion to the stone pathway, face up, his mouth frozen open with surprise.

Seeing my opening, I dove for my weapon, I grabbed and then rolled over and fired 2 rounds at each of the other minions. Their heads exploded and danced an eerie dance as their bodies jerked and they collapsed on the ground. I wanted to shoot at Morgan's attackers, but she seemed to have the situation well in hand. I saw the attacker who held her arm behind her back's head explode. His accomplice was momentarily distracted by all the shooting which allowed Morgan to put her foot where she thought it would do the best. He howled in real agony, even I flinched when I saw what she had done to him. He doubled over in pain and Morgan grabbed him by the head and slammed her knee into his upper face. I could hear the crack of the cartilage and saw blood flowing. She bent over, picked up her pistol and grabbed him by the hair.

"Look at me. You remember you asked me what I was going to do about you pawing on me?" Morgan screamed. She knew she already had one in the chamber as she pressed the pistol against the minion's head. "Here's your answer, bitch." She squeezed off two rounds and his head exploded and sprayed her with a spray of blood. She let go of his hair and his body fell to the ground, blood beginning to leak over the pathway.

Herr Steele had been momentarily paralyzed by what he had just witnessed. He recovered and started to flee, but lost his footing. He landed face down in the path, his arms spread out wide. Morgan approached behind me. I used my foot to roll him over on his back. I looked down at him. He was no longer in charge and he knew it. He laid there cringing. It was disgusting.

"Look, Colonel Steele, we both know the documents you tried to pass off on me were fake. Tell me the truth and I'll let you live. Where is Caesar's Medallion.?"

He looked shocked that I addressed him as Colonel. He made gulping noises, the kind you would hear from a fish out of water but remained silent. He then sputtered, "Please don't hurt me, I'm an old man. I'll tell you anything you want. If I help you, you must protect me from them. I beg of you." I was never in the STASSI. I swear it's all lies created by my enemies. Please help me," he babbled in terror.

I looked down at him and said grimly, "You're a liar. Last chance, Colonel Steele."

"Inside my coat pocket, I have money and airplane tickets to where I was supposed to meet up with our group. I was ordered to eliminate you at first."

I could see his lips trembling. I opened his overcoat and pulled out a large amount of Argentine cash and tickets to Mar del Plata. It was so quiet now. I could hear Morgan breathing behind me.

"Did you have a location where you were you supposed to meet these people?"

"No, they were going to contact me at my hotel. Please show me mercy. I told you everything I knew. You said you would help me," he whined.

Morgan whispered to me, "If it was up to me, I'd kill the dirty bastard. Think of all the souls he tortured when he was in STASSI. He showed them no mercy. For Christ sake, he was going to kill us. I'll back your play whatever it is, Miller. I know you know that."

I nodded and whispered back, "I know."

Colonel Steele spat in Morgan's general direction, "The bitch is crazy. Don't listen to her, he screamed. She will betray you. She loves to kill. She got off when she butchered that poor boy... You saw what she did. I never intended to harm you Herr Rixey, I had to kill that murderous bitch. She is working against us. You need me to help you complete your mission, not a dirty whore like her."

The anger in Steele's face quickly faded into a brief smile. His eyes that had been full of disgust just seconds before seem to look upon me with admiration. "Herr Rixey, you would have made a fine officer in STASSI ... you would have been one of the best."

I thought about it and made my decision. It all happened so quickly. Somewhat bothered by all that had happened and all I had done; I paused and pulled my map of the Cemetery out of my pocket. Morgan had joined me by then. I pointed to our goal, Eva Peron's burial monument. "We should be there in a couple of minutes," I said my voice devoid of any emotion.

Morgan took my arm and cooed, "Miller you did the right thing.

Was I the good man that Banner said I was? Had I really done the right thing as Morgan had suggested? Was I really the man Steele said I was? I couldn't be sure who was closer to the truth.

The walk to Peron vault was peaceful in an odd sort of way. All we could hear the was the steady beating of the rain on us and on the various buildings. No more gunfire or screaming. I actually enjoyed it. We had been fortunate that the night weather had been so terrible and the sky so dark. Apparently, no one had heard us or if they had, showed good sense in avoiding the area. I knew the bodies we had left behind would not be discovered until morning. Suddenly, I realized we had a problem that was certain to develop once the bodies were found in the morning. I cannot think of a single situation where is it either wise or prudent to carrying weapons involved in multiple killings. This did not seem to be an exception to the rule. I reached into my pocket and pulled out my phone and once it was ready, I dialed a number.

"Kaplan Cleaning Company."

"The password is swordfish1236."

I heard some keys clicking in the background. "Yes sir, Mr. Rixey, how can we assist you?"

"I have a Glock-17 that needs to be replaced. It was involved in an incident where several people were shot and killed." My partner needs a..."

Morgan mouthed, "A Sig Sauer P 229 Legion."

"My partner needs a Sig Sauer P 229 Legion. Will providing those weapons be a problem?"

"Certainly not Mr. Rixey. Your location, please?"

I mentioned the hotel that we were staying at as well as the room number.

"We have an employee who will be able to provide those weapons for you at cost plus a delivery charge which currently works in the Buenos Aires area. We can have them delivered to your hotel in about ninety minutes. Any delivery instructions?"

"Yes. Just have them left in our hotel mailbox. We will pick them up when we get back there."

"You will be handling the destruction of the weapons, Mr. Rixey?"

"Yes. Quite right. Bill the office and since I am out of town, please don't change the password.

"Excellent sir." I heard a click.

"Wow, handsome, smart, and clever. You're quite a package," Morgan said with a giggle. "Good thinking about the weapons. It would have been challenging to explain to the police what we were doing with weapons involved in multiple killings."

I smiled at her, "Thanks."

"Wow, handsome, smart, and clever. You're quite a package," Morgan said with a giggle. "Good thinking about the weapons."

I smiled at her, "Thanks."

We finished our trek to the burial monument. I pulled my flashlight as we walked to the back. I clicked it on and there was the raised engraving of Caesar's Medallion.

I turned to Morgan as I pointed at the engraving, "Any thoughts how this works or if it works at all?"

Morgan studied the design, "No idea at all."

"Morgan get out your flashlight. I am going to try something that I doubt works, but you never know." I crouched down and pressed the engraving, it sank into the stone, but there was still access to the rounded part. I made three full turns to the right and then three full turns to the left. I pressed the engraving into the stone and heard a clock, followed by a rumble as a previously invisible door began to open. The creaking seemed so loud, but I realized it was amplified by the silence of the night. Finally, a five foot by five-foot opening appeared. I checked my magazine. Only a couple of rounds left. I pushed on the button that released it and slapped in a fresh one. I pulled the slide back to put one in the chamber. I took a deep breath and began to make my way into the crypt.

I shined my light into the dark entrance and saw a stairway that went down. How far down, I had no idea. "Watch your step," I said to Morgan. We began our descent.

We went down two flights of stairs and we finally reached a room. I swept my flashlight around the room. I could feel Morgan's breath on the back of my neck. I finally saw what I had been looking for, Eva Peron's final place of rest. I approached the glass-covered coffin. I kicked a small bag that made a jingly noise. I was hoping to find some type of clue in this room. I shone the light into her coffin, it was empty!

Chapter Twenty-two

"How often have I told you that when you have eliminated the impossible, whatever remains, no matter how improbable is the truth.
Sherlock Holmes in The Sign of the Four

I was stunned when I saw the empty casket. Morgan had crept up behind me and I could feel her warm breath on my neck.

"What the hell is going on? She is supposed to be buried here for all eternity?" Morgan asked.

I stood there, trying to make sense of the entire occurrence. I blinked to make sure I wasn't hallucinating. I wasn't.

I found my voice, "Well, it's pretty basic. Either someone stole her body or she has risen from the dead to lead her "shirtless ones," her fanatical followers, on a revolution against the current Argentine regime."

"Raised from the dead? What a bunch of crap."

I sighed and shook my head from what we hadn't found. This was not going as I had hoped for.

I bounced my flashlight all over the walls of the crypt. Nothing showed up except some fine engravings. No doors appeared, secret or otherwise.

"Is it? Someone in the Argentine government was concerned about it. She died in 1952 and wasn't allowed to remain buried in her country until 1978. The Argentine government oversaw the security to make sure the crypt was impenetrable from either outside or inside. They almost succeeded." I turned around to face her, "Can you imagine the reaction that will occur when the word of her body being gone gets out to the public?"

Morgan bent over and picked up the bag I had kicked. She gave it a heft and I heard some jingling.

"Put that bag in your pocket. We can look at it later. We need to get out of here and out the Cemetery quickly. I don't want to be around when the locals discover our handiwork."

We headed up the stairs and upon exiting, turned our flashlights off. I closed the entrance to the tomb by reversing the previous movements I had done to get the door open. I saw the door shudder and heard it making creaking noises as it slowly closed.

We quickly headed back to the hotel. The weather had not gotten any better since we had entered the crypt. We both had our weapons rapidly broken down and began dumping parts of them as we left the Cemetery.

Morgan retook my arm and cocked her head. "You know, you made a pretty good guess back there at the crypt as to how to open the door. How did you figure that out? I'm not sure I would have."

"Thanks, it was basically figuring out how to spin the dial. The number of times was easy. Hitler and other top Nazis were into mysticism. The number three is very big in that area. Lots of religions use it to show good fortune or other favorable things. Consider Christianity, three men on the cross when Christ died, The Father, The Son, and The Holy Ghost, and even the Three Wise Men."

I paused as we walked on, the rain was falling harder. "The way in had to be simple, easy to remember, and capable of being quickly executed. I made an educated guess and we got rewarded."

We both had finished disposing of our weapons and were only about five minutes from the hotel. We were both soaked and I am sure looked like what the cat had dragged in. To top it off, I knew we would be getting a visit from Inspector Gomez tomorrow once the identities of the men who were dead in the Cemetery were discovered. I had a case to solve and did not want to end up being held answering a lot of fool questions. I wasn't thrilled.

Morgan asked, "Miller, what's your best theory on the missing body? There seems to be a lot of explanations."

The rain started to pour harder and I guided us to a building with an overhang to wait out the worst of the storm.

"Okay, well for starters I am not ready to believe Eva Peron rose from the dead. That leaves three possible alternatives. First, they took her body for cloning. Even with the advanced scientists, the Nazis had, to me it seems fantastic that they could have made that much progress in the field. The second is they have taken photographs of her empty tomb to use as a signal to her peasant followers that it was time for the revolution to begin. With social media and fake news, all sorts of sightings of her could be reported of her leading troops and other things. Even though she has been dead over sixty years, she is still highly revered in some circles so she would be highly valued as a symbol for revolutionary types."

She asked impatiently, "Number three?"

"What if when she died, someone hid an object in her body for safe keeping. They couldn't have foreseen the problems they were going to have to keep the body in the country. Remember, she was only finally laid to rest in Argentina in 1978. They were probably concerned about the logistics of stealing the body and then transporting it back here for examination and removal of the hidden item. All my guesses seem thin, but this seems the least thin of the set."

"It may be thin, but it makes sense to me."

I looked up at the sky and saw the rain was abating. "We should get a move on. The rain is letting up. I have no urge to either be stuck out here all night or be soaked when we begin walking again."

We got some very strange looks as we climbed up the steps to the hotel. The doorman sort of smiled at us as he held the door for us. I noticed some of the odd looks we received from the various guests as we approached the front desk in the lobby.

Maria looked up and seemed nonplussed by our appearances. She shooed some bellhops away from the front desk area before turning her attention to us, "Good evening Señor and Señora. How can I help you?"

I smiled at her, "Do you ever get a day off?"

"No Señor Rixey. I was promoted to Assistant Manager for my handling of that situation that occurred earlier this morning."

I felt a familiar painful and hurry up, we got things to do type squeeze on my arm courtesy of Morgan. I glared at Morgan and she responded by sweetly smiling back at me. I couldn't win. "Um, well congrats on the promotion and is there anything for 796?"

She checked our box and brought back a small box, an envelope with our hotel's logo embossed on it, and a cablegram. I thanked her and we headed toward the elevator, with Morgan releasing her grip on my arm as we neared the elevator.

I knew what was in the box, the two pistols I had asked for from Kaplan. I wished I could have used their disposal service for the bodies we had left behind in the Cemetery. That was simply not an option for me in Buenos Aires. I knew they just maintained a small office down here for little assignments such as weapon replacement or supplying. I opened the cablegram. I already knew it was from Willard and when I opened it and saw a series of two-digit numbers, I knew that it would have to wait until we got back to our room. I opened the envelope and began to read: "I was very happy to have evened out the odds. You and Morgan make a very devastating team. I saw you two disappear and then reappear and then leave. I then called a local cleaning company. They will tend to your mess. We really need to get together sometime. Please feel free to contact me if I can help aid your enjoyment of Argentina. S/ K. Dinisi."

The elevator stopped with a lurch and the door opened as the bell rung signifying our arrival on the seventh floor. I handed the letter to Morgan who read it with some amusement.

"Miller, you seem to have some very unusual friends as well as unusual resources. Don't get me wrong, I am sure glad you have both. To me, it just adds your character." She giggled, "Perhaps a drink when we get inside?"

I nodded as I unlocked our suite door. We entered. I made a gesture to Morgan and she nodded and went to her room and brought back the wand. I collapsed on the couch, took what I had taken from Steele out of my jacket pocket and laid it on the table. I dropped my soaked hat and jacket on the floor. I reached for my bag and cipher wheel to begin decoding the message.

Morgan came out of my room and finished checking our living room area. She gave an all-clear sign. I looked up at her as I had just finished decoding the message. She could tell I was not very happy.

"What's wrong, Miller?"

"We got what we call a major-league problem. Here, look at this."

I handed her the translation: ***F-R-O-M L-A-Y-N-E S-T-E-E-L-E H-I-G-H L-E-V-E-L R-E-S-O-U-R-C-E P-R-O-T-E-C-T A-T A-L-L C-O-S-T. W-B*** **B**

Chapter Twenty-three

"Truth is ever to be found in simplicity, and not in the multiplicity and confusion of things." Isaac Newton

This case seemed to be getting more and more confusing. Each turn of events seemed to raise new questions. Was Steele really a double agent working for the U.S.? If so, why didn't he mention that as he laid on the ground pleading for his life? I know it's something I would have done.

Morgan snapped me out of my reverie. Her eyes widened as she finished reading Willard's cable, "You sure about this?"

I nodded, "Quite sure. I mean I'm sure that I translated the cable correctly, I'm not buying that Steele was working for the government. If things had been left up to him, we would be dead."

Morgan got up, went to the balcony and opened the sliding door. "I love the sound of rainstorms," she said somewhat distractedly. She turned back toward me, "I agree, Steele was not really working for the government. I like the triple agent theory."

I smiled, "So do I, but just the sounds, not being in it."

She stopped at the room minifridge, opened the door and pulled out two bottles of beer. She handed me one as she sat back down, "The drink I promised," she said with a soft laugh. I nodded my thanks.

I've been giving this some thought. It seemed like every time we ran into him, he had bad intentions for us. That's not the way friends treat other friends."

"It sure doesn't."

"What are we supposed to do about Herr Steele. I mean there is going to be hell to raise when word of what happened gets out. This sounds like we will be getting a visit from the police as soon as they are discovered. I mean, that's what I would do. You have the initial run-in with Steele at the airport and now Steele and one of the guys from the meeting is lying dead with their heads blown off?"

"Word is never getting out, Ms. Dinisi has taken care of that problem once she called the cleaners. By now, there is no trace of anything left. With any luck, Herr Steele is lying at the bottom of a vat filled with quick lime."

I took a sip of the beer, "One thing bothers me. If Steele was really working for the U.S., why not mention that in an attempt to save his life?"

"Well, that's the million-dollar question. It should have been his ace in the hole, but he never did. Maybe it was the stress and the pressure of the situation? Perhaps he was legitimate and saw you initially and me later as enemies out to stop the assignment he was working on? I guess we will never know," Morgan sighed.

I reached over to the table and picked up all I had taken off from Herr Steele. One thing that struck me odd was there was no set of keys. No keys to a house, no keys to a car, and no keys to a safety deposit box. All that was in his wallet was ten thousand pesos and a New York driver's license. The license identified him as Herman Steele. He had a card key to a hotel room, but without any identification as to the room number. It did have the name of the hotel prominently displayed though. Pretty standard hotel security. It renders the key worthless unless you happen to know the correct room number. If the guest reports it as lost or stolen, it's deactivated and no longer works on any door. I opened the envelope, saw a stack of local currency and an American passport. The passport also verified his identity as Herman Steele. I opened up his airplane ticket. He was not scheduled to leave until the day after tomorrow. The ticket was round trip from Buenos Aries to Mar Del Plata with an open return date. The open return told me he had no idea how long his reason for being in Mar Del Plata was going to be.

"I found thirty thousand pesos. Any chance we can retire on that?" I showed Morgan Steele's American passport.

Morgan looked at the passport and shook her head, "You are

looking at about two thousand dollars American. Basically, walking around money for a man like Steele."

"It looks like Mar Del Plata is our next stop. What can you tell me about that city?"

"It's about 260 miles from Buenos Aires. It's a pretty nice town. Many of the wealthy Argentines have a summer home there. It's pretty easy to get there. I mean it's only an hour flight."

I shook my head, "No. Airplanes are a bad idea. We won't be able to carry our weapons on a flight. I also would like to stay clear of the airport until we have to leave."

"There is a train that leaves Buenos Aires from Plaza Constitution Station at 5:30 this afternoon. It typically gets to Mar Del Plata around 11:30." Morgan wrinkled her nose, "We could drive, but that would not be my best choice. I've taken the train before, it's a lovely trip."

"The train sounds good. So, you said they have a fair number of wealthy Argentines who have summer homes there? What about tourists?"

"Oh, plenty of tourists. People like it once they have tired of the hustle and bustle of Buenos Aires. We would blend in quite nicely."

"Okay, the train it is. Even though we will be gone for a day or two, I want to keep this room. If we hang a do not disturb sign on the door, that should keep the staff out. Now, what I would like for you to do is to verify the reservation for Herr Steele. I have a feeling that this card key we found on him wasn't for where he was staying in Buenos Aires. I'm guessing he is using that hotel room as his base of operations during his trip there. I am pretty sure he has used whatever room that key would unlock. I didn't find any references to a reservation on him. I'm hoping I'm right."

Morgan nodded, "Should be easy enough to find out, I mean hotel sites are usually super easy to crack. I have a friend who can have our information pretty quickly." Morgan started to rise.

"One more question, what's security going to be like at the train station? With the airport shootings, will that cause them to increase security? I really don't want to go down there unarmed."

"Practically nonexistent on the outside. When I was out earlier, I checked the train station out myself. I was curious about that same issue. No changes that I could see. When we board our train since it's the train many of the wealthy and the tourists take, only a cursory inspection. I doubt we will even be stopped."

Morgan returned fifteen minutes later and was smiling. "Herr Steele is staying in Room 442. You were right, Miller. He has had that same room for the past three months. Who knows, maybe we will find something useful in the room?"

"Yeah, we should have time for a decent search. We will be down there before he was supposed to leave. That means his contacts shouldn't be around either."

Morgan nodded, "I'm going to shower then go to bed. I'll see you later on. I think it's safe to say we both had a pretty full day." I waved her good night.

I called down to the front desk and to my delight, I found out that the concierge was still available. When I had hung up, we had our train tickets and the hotel room across the hall from a Herr Steele.

I smiled in satisfaction as I pulled a fresh cigar from my pocket humidor. After the usual rituals, I lit it. I sat back, enjoying the fact that it seemed like finally, I was ahead of the game. As far as I knew, the local bad guys were dead and we had what appeared to be a solid lead on the location of the Medallion. Other than the broken door at the Cemetery, there was no trace of what had happened earlier in the evening. It looked like we were covered. Life was good again.

I started to get up to look in the hotel minibar for something better to drink than beer. I couldn't find my preferred tipple, Macallan, but found an adequate substitute. One must make sacrifices when on the job. I open the ice bucket and scooped out a few cubes and tossed them in a glass. I would have never dared to ice with Macallan, that would have been sacrilegious. My cell phone rang. I looked at the number on caller ID and did not recognize it. I answered it anyway.

"Miller, this is Bobby. We have a crisis that needs your immediate attention. This is the top priority."

Chapter Twenty-four

"The darkest places in hell are reserved for those who maintain their neutrality in times of moral crisis." Dante Alighieri

Based on Willard's cable and what had happened earlier at the Cemetery, I had a pretty good idea what Bobby's crisis was. Steele had obviously missed a check-in call.

"Bobby, unless the crisis is involving Caesar's Medallion, I am much too busy to take on another case or assignment."

Bobby sputtered, "It does. One of my employees, Herman Steele, has gone missing. He is late for his check-in call. He told me he had made contact with you and was helping you on the case. It is of the utmost importance that I can contact immediately. In addition to helping you, he was working on something just for me."

"Yes, a German fellow. Seemed like a nice enough guy. We had met a few times, most recently for drinks in the hotel lounge. He seemed capable, I am just sure something came up and he missed the call."

Bobby pleaded, "I could really use your help on this, Miller. I mean this cannot take too much of your time, right?"

I was about to tell him to buzz off, but then I was struck with a brilliant idea. "You know Bobby, I suppose I could take a little time and check around. Any idea where he was staying down here?"

Bobby gave me the name an address of the hotel that Steele had been staying at. The hotel was in Buenos Aries. I made of a note of it, confident that Morgan would be able to find it easily enough. Judging by his frantic tone of voice, I was sure he would agree to almost anything I asked. I really wanted to search that room and needed the key.

"Okay. Can you get me his room number? If I don't find him right away that would be a big help. Also, I am going to need either a key card or some other way to gain access to his room. Can you do that?"

"Yes, Miller. My company is paying the hotel bill, so I don't foresee any problems. I will get you on a list that will allow you access to the room. I don't expect any problems doing that. I will have to wait until the manager comes in, but you will be able to get in the room later this morning. Will that work for you?"

"Yeah. That will be fine. I will have a report for you by mid-afternoon at the latest."

I could hear the relief in his voice, "Thank you very much. I really appreciate this. There will be something extra for you."

I smiled to myself, "Glad to help. Just make sure I can have access to the room when I get there. I probably won't need it, but you can never tell. Also, if Steele calls, let me know so I can change my plans."

"I will handle it personally. Once again, thank you, Miller."

"Always glad to help, Bobby. I am hanging up now. Have a good evening." I did a fist pump after hanging up. Talk about having something dropped in your lap.

The fact that I was dead tired hit me hard. I was still slightly jet lagged. That in combination with the past few days' activities and the two drinks I just had finally had caught up with me.

I knew the next few days were going to be just as busy as the previous ones. I finished what was left of my drink, hit the shower, and was asleep before my head hit the pillow.

Chapter Twenty-five

"Men, in general, are quick to believe that which they wish to be true."
Julius Caesar

I had just led the Detroit Lions to their first-ever Super Bowl victory. I was being hoisted on the shoulders of my exuberant teammates. In the background, I could hear a knocking sound and a female voice. As I slowly regained consciousness, the dream had faded away and I heard Morgan's voice.

"Time to get up, Miller."

Still a little groggy, I mumbled, "I am now."

"You decent?"

"More or less."

The door opened as Morgan bounded into the room. She was dressed and looked ready to take on the new day. "Come on and get up."

"You had a chance to watch any news yet?"

"Yes. The break-in at La Recoleta got minimal coverage. The Airport Shootings are still basically getting wall to wall coverage."

"Guess what happened after you went to bed?"

"Someone stopped by and delivered the Medallion to you?"

I laughed, "Not quite. I got a call from Bobby. He wants me to investigate the disappearance of Herr Steele. It seems like Steele missed a check-in call last night. He wants to know if he is simply AWOL or something bad happened to him."

Morgan became very enthusiastic, "Wow, what a great break for us and a bad break for Steele. We will be able to search two of his rooms and maybe really bring this case to a close. When do we leave for his Buenos Aires hotel?"

"Soon, I need to get dressed and then grab a bite to eat. I'll meet you in the lobby restaurant in about twenty minutes." I gave her the address of the hotel. "You got any idea of where it's located?"

"It's about ten minutes from here. Normally we could walk it, but with the rain continuing, I'll get a cab. I will give José a call. You know the guy from last night."

On my way to the restaurant, I stopped at the front desk, "Anything for 796?"

"Sorry, Señor. Nothing today."

I nodded, "The Señora and I will be out site seeing and won't be back for a few days. We intend to keep our room."

"That will not be a problem, Señor." He made a note. "Just inform us when you return."

I continued to the restaurant where Morgan and I ate. I paid our bill and we were off. The rain had picked up in its intensity. We could hear it even from inside the lobby. A doorman greeted us as he opened the door.

"Good morning Señor and Señora, may I get you a cab?"

I handed him a small Argentine bill, "No thanks, we have a cab waiting." I pointed to an old battered white Chevy minivan."

"Very good Señor. Enjoy your day."

We headed to the cab, José was already out holding the door with one hand and an umbrella in another. He nodded toward the both of us and said in a combination of broken English and Spanish, "Greetings *la jeffe*."

Morgan nodded and gave him the address. The cab took off with a lurch and some protesting squeals. As the taxi hurtled toward its destination, Morgan turned to me and said, "I'm going to give him orders to wait for us. I doubt he will mind considering what we will be paying him for this ride."

I laughed, "I somehow doubt it too."

Traffic was light and despite the bad weather, José drove with his usual reckless abandon and we were soon in the circle drive of the hotel. Morgan and I got out of the cab. We watched José pull up to a waiting area and then we went inside. We quickly made it to the front desk area. No guests were standing there, only a couple of very bored bellhops. We caught the eye of a young, rather thin and swarthy person working behind the desk.

"Good morning Señor and Señora. How may I help you today?"

I eyed his nametag, it read Ricardo Ruiz: General Manager.

"Señor Ruiz, have you been in touch with a Bobby Layne from America?"

"Why yes. He called about an hour ago, are you by any chance the famous American detective, Señor Miller Rixey that he talked about? He said you would be by there around this time."

"I'm not sure how famous, but I am Señor Rixey, the American detective." I produced my passport.

As Ruiz glanced at it, he said, "Yes. Señor Layne said you would be by checking up on Senior Steele." He hesitated.

"Is there a problem?"

"Yes, Señor. Señor Layne said you would need access to his room. Even though Señor Layne's company is paying for the room and he authorized your entry, I cannot allow you access to the room. We have very strict laws about allowing strangers into other guest's rooms. Unless you have the proper paperwork, I am sorry I cannot let you in." He shrugged helplessly. "My hands are tied Señor. One moment, Señor." He answered the phone and briefly chatted and then hung up. He looked at me almost apologetically.

I couldn't believe it. I was this close to perhaps unraveling this case and I was being stopped by some law that didn't make any sense to me. I turned to Morgan and saw her removing an envelope from her jacket.

"Señor, I think I might have the proper paperwork that you need," she said.

Chapter Twenty-six

"Knowing is not enough; we must apply. Willing is not enough; we must do." Johann Wolfgang von Goethe

He grinned wolfishly at Morgan, "Yes Señora?"

Morgan handed him an envelope with the symbol of our hotel embossed on it, "You will find the proper paperwork in here."

Ruiz looked inside the envelope briefly and did a double take. The envelope quickly vanished inside one of his jacket pockets. He smiled again, showing all of his teeth. "Everything now appears to be in order, Señor." He reached under the counter, pulled a key card and ran it through the encoding machine. He then slid it into an envelope and wrote 597 on the outside. As he handed it to me, he asked, "Will you be needing any assistance in finding this room, Señor?

"No thank you. We can find our way."

We headed toward the elevator banks. "What the hell was that with papers?"

"Oh? Well I always like to be prepared. I figured there was a good chance of a shakedown. I also knew we needed to get into the room. So, I gave him 3000 Pesos that we had relieved Steele of. I did it in a manner that allowed him to keep his honor."

I nodded, "Everyone thinks they are underpaid and even the corrupt don't want their honor challenged. Willard taught me that some time back. Very discretely done, by the way."

We arrived at the elevator banks, stepped into an open door and pressed five. We rode up in silence and the elevator stopped with a jerk. A bell rang and the door opened. We stepped out and much to our delight, the room was only a few steps from the elevator.

I motioned Morgan to pull her weapon. I waited until she has screwed the suppressor into the barrel. I unlocked the room door and we pushed our way in. The room had been trashed. Mattresses had been slashed, every dresser drawer had been emptied, chairs had been slashed and overturned. Someone had been very thorough in their search it looked like. I stood there looking dumbfounded. My attention was drawn to the room phone as it began ringing. Should I answer it or let it ring and get the hell out of here?

Chapter Twenty-seven

"Human behavior flows from three main sources: desire, emotion, and knowledge." Plato

I made a decision. Not answering the phone didn't seem like an option. It could be the manager calling or it could be a bad guy. If it was a bad guy, we should still have time to clear the room before they got their forces up here.

I picked up the phone, "Herman?"

"Bobby, this is an unsecured line. Why the hell are you calling me on this number? Are you crazy?"

"No Miller. I was hoping to contact Herman. What are you doing in his room?"

"Hang up and call me on my cell." I clicked off to end any further discussion.

I heard my phone ring. I pressed answer and after a series of clicks, I saw the secured light flicker off and on and then stop. My line was secured. "Bobby, Herman isn't here and I think we both knew that."

"Miller, I thought he would be up there."

"Did you forget our conversation last night? You asked Morgan and me to look for Steele? You got us access to his room? Ring a bell? He isn't and his room has been trashed by someone looking for something. Morgan and I had just entered his room when we heard the phone ringing."

"What do you recommend we do?"

"It's what you are going to do," I said pointedly. "Bobby, when I leave here, I am going to hang a do not disturb sign on the door. That will give you time to make some sort of arrangement as to how to get this room fixed and keep the police and hotel staff out of it. Can you do that?"

"Yes, I can do that."

"Then do it. I'll call you back if we find anything." I clicked off before Bobby could offer another excuse or complaint. He knew what needed to be done.

I saw a message light flashing on the room phone. I picked up the receiver and pressed the button. The message was in Spanish. I saved it and hung up.

I turned to say something to Morgan, but ever the professional, she had already begun searching areas that may have been missed by the earlier searchers, vents and light fixtures. I could hear the soft whirring sounds coming from the bathroom area.

"We need to get out of here. You have any luck?"

"Give me a minute. I'm almost done."

I found a seat amidst the rubble and waited. I heard a squeal of delight come from the bathroom and saw Morgan bound out of there waving two envelopes, one thick and one thin. "Look what I found." She joined me where I was sitting.

"That Steele was pretty sharp. You couldn't even tell that the vent had been removed and replaced." She nodded in approval. "I probably couldn't have even got the vent open without my little drill." She smiled.

I pointed to the phone. "There's a message for Steele on there, it's in Spanish."

Morgan got up from where we had been seated. She walked to the phone, picked up the receiver and pressed the message button. She pressed the save button and turned to me, "It was verifying a restaurant reservation."

"Okay. Well, let's get out of here and check out the envelopes in a safer place." I found a do not disturb sign that I hung on the door as I heard it click shut behind us. The room phone began ringing.

I looked at Morgan, "There's no one calling that number that I want to talk to."

We walked to the bank of elevators. I started to push the button and then stopped.

I looked up and saw on the floor indicator somebody was on their way up. Where they were heading, I couldn't be sure, but my guess was one of them was coming to our floor and was interested in Herr Steele's room. I grabbed Morgan and said, "Stairs, now."

We sped toward the stairway entrance. Luckily for us, the entrance could not be seen from the elevators. I heard a gentle tinkle of the elevator announcing its presence on the floor. This was quickly followed by loud voices and pounding on what I was pretty sure was Steele's door. I quietly pulled open the door open and gently shut it behind us. As we hurried down the stairs to the lobby, the noise vanished. I was gassed by the time we reached the lobby entrance, naturally, Morgan had not even broken a sweat.

We collected ourselves and tried our best to look like an average couple. We locked arms and slowly walked through the lobby. The doorman greeted us as he opened the door. I nodded and tipped him as we stepped out into the rain.

We saw José's cab still sitting where he had parked it before we went inside. He must have seen us coming out of the building as he had the rear cab door opened for us. As we got into the cab, Morgan said something to him, handed him a wad of cash, and we were soon back at our hotel.

The doorman greeted us cheerfully and opened the door for us. I breathed a sigh of relief. Safe at last. We had avoided a major disaster by only a mere few minutes. I didn't want to get involved with that crew that had just arrived at Steele's room. My relief was short-lived as I looked at the front desk and saw an angry looking Inspector Ramirez glaring at me. He motioned for us to come to the desk. What the Inspector wants, the Inspector gets, at least in Argentina.

Chapter Twenty-eight

"Truth will ultimately prevail where there is pains to bring it to light."
George Washington

When a man like Inspector Ramirez summons you, you go. Morgan and I approached the front desk. "Hello, Inspector. How is your day going?" I smarmed.

Ramirez growled, "It seems like my day would have been much better if you had never come to Argentina, much less Buenos Aires."

Putting on my best hurt feelings face, "Why whatever is that supposed to mean?"

The Inspector held up his beefy hand and counted off, "First we have the shootings at the airport. You were present. Second, there was the so-called attempted robbery of your hotel room that resulted in two dead Americans. Third, a man you were seen quarreling with at the airport has been reported missing. Finally, I cannot prove this, but I have a feeling that somehow you and the lovely Señora were responsible for the breaking at our revered Cemetery."

He paused to take a breath while I silently cursed Bobby. I was sure he had been the one who had called the authorities about Herr Steele being missing.

"Señor Rixey, you seem to attract trouble the way steel is attracted to metal." He shook his head. "I don't believe in chances occurrences. I will be keeping my eye on you and the lovely Señora."

I didn't like where this was heading, "Look, Inspector, I am a victim of circumstances. I have committed no crimes and have no knowledge of any of these occurrences, nor the motivation behind the robbery attempt."

Morgan spoke up, "Inspector, my husband and I are leaving your lovely city for a few days to tour Mar Del Plata. I have heard such nice things about it."

Ramirez turned to Morgan and actually smiled, "That's wonderful news Señora. Please feel free to stay down there some extra days as there is so much to see."

He turned to me, smile gone, "Señor Rixey, will it be necessary for me to inform my friends on the Mar Del Plata Police about your arrival?"

"No, sir. I don't expect any problems down there. None at all."

He sighed, "Why do I doubt that?" He smiled at Morgan and glowered at me as he headed out of the lobby.

Chapter Twenty-nine

"Never complain and never explain." Benjamin Disraeli

After checking for any mail for our room, Morgan and I headed back to our suite. Only the monotonous music coming from a speaker in the elevator, combined with the whirring of the elevator as it headed for its goal broke the silence. We soon arrived at our floor and I took out my card key. Out of the corner of my eye, I saw Morgan draw her pistol. I nodded to her and pushed the door open as I slid in the card key. Everything was as we left it. I took a seat on the couch as Morgan began her search for eavesdropping devices that had been planted while we were gone.

The leather bag Morgan had found in the crypt was still lying on the table in front of the couch. I opened the bag and saw inside what appeared to be gold coins. I went to the minibar and grabbed a towel off of it so I could handle the coins without getting my fingerprints and body acids on them. As an experienced numismatist, I knew that nothing can damage coins quicker than fingerprints and body acids. I gingerly removed all twenty coins from the bag and laid them down on the table. I examined the obverse and saw a picture of a German eagle, but saw a date on the coin that troubled me. I flipped the coins over and saw a Nazi swastika. I sighed and shook my head.

Morgan appeared back in the living room and saw the coins on the table. "Cool looking, are they worth anything?"

"Nope, all fakes. Gold plated by some crook who would typically sell them to coin collectors who don't know anything about Nazi coinage. While the Nazis stole a lot of gold, none of it ever went into coinage."

I could see a look of disappointment on her face, "You know this how?"

"I've been collecting coins since I was a boy. A few years ago, I was thinking about expanding my collection to include German coins. I never did, but the research stuck. I pointed to the date on the coins, this was the last year the Nazis even used silver to mint coins. After that, it was zinc and aluminum. The other metals were too valuable for the war e ffort. Sorry, Morgan, all we have here is a bag full of junk. Small wonder that they forgot it."

I lit a cigar, "So did you get a chance to check out the envelopes you found?"

She took a seat next to me, "I was just about to check that out. She dropped the thicker envelope on the table and we both heard a thud. She reached for the thin envelope opened it up and got a strange look on her face as she began to read it to me:

"To the Finder of this Letter: If you are reading this, I am either dead or no longer in a position to complete the task I am asking you to perform. The fact that you found this envelope means you are brilliant and resourceful as I had it well hidden. Inside the other envelope are 1.5 Million Dollars of Bearer Bonds. After deducting 100,000 for your time and trouble, please deliver the remainder to my niece, Karin Steele. Her address is listed below. I have not seen her for fifteen years since she was three. I am unable to describe her to you. She will recognize a gold signet ring that is in the other envelope as she used to love to play with it when we visited. She has no knowledge of my work in the STASI or anything else in my career. S/ Herman Steele."

Morgan sighed as she folded over the letter. She reached for the thicker envelope and as she opened it up, a heavy gold signet ring bearing a gothic "S" fell out. She looked inside the envelope and pulled out some certificates. She quickly counted them. "Just like the letter said, there are fifteen of them here and each is worth 100,000 Dollars apiece."

"You sure they are good?"

"Yeah, they seem to be. Issued by our Treasury Department and I doubt Herr Steele would be giving his niece phony bearer bonds."

I picked up the ring and hefted it. "Very nice and I am sure very valuable." I turned to face Morgan, "Even a scumbag can have his good side, I guess. Here's what I want to do, if the niece seems on the level, give her the entire amount. If she isn't, we will deal with that when we find out otherwise. You said you had her address?"

"Yeah. She lives in Mar Del Plata."

"How convenient. We can make that our first stop tomorrow. How old is the letter?"

"About ten days old."

I nodded, "Good, her address will be current."

"You aren't holding back the 100,000 Herr Steele said we could?"

I shook my head, "Call me a romantic, it doesn't seem right. I would take $100,000 from Layne or the government and not even break a sweat. But. . . "

Morgan reached over and gave me a hug, "Miller that's so sweet of you."

I returned her hug, enjoying the feeling.

"Now let's get packed and ready to go. Give José a call and we can head for the train station."

We spent the next half hour getting packed and checking and filling our magazines. I gathered up the bearer bonds and the ring, placing the ring in my pants pocket the bonds in my bag I took one last look around the room and went to the balcony to make sure the glass door was shut and locked.

We headed for the lobby and were greeted by the doorman, "May I get you and your lovely wife a cab?"

I shook my head as I slipped him a couple of two-peso coins, "No thanks. We have one waiting."

He tipped his cap and we stood under the awning waiting until we saw José's cab pull into the hotel drive. He got out of the car and held the door for us as we scampered in and took our seats. I heard Morgan tell him where we were going and we were off.

As we pulled out of the driveway, I noticed a black SUV with very dark tinted windows begin to follow us immediately. The driver of the SUV kept a perfect distance behind us. I realized it wasn't my being paranoid that we were being followed when we made two turns and the SUV made both turns and continued to keep a measured distance from our cab. We arrived at the train station and stopped. As we got out of the cab, I noticed an older heavyset man get out of the SUV that had been trailing us. He produced a badge, "Señor and Señora Rixey, a moment of your time please?"

Chapter Thirty

"Life is really simple, but we insist on making it complicated." Confucius

I rolled my eyes as the officer approached. I knew there was no way I would stand up to a search. I was armed, had a dead man's ring in my pocket, and $1,500,000 worth of bearer bonds on me and no reasonable explanation for why I had what I had. I motioned for Morgan to stay put and decided to take the advantage. I began walking toward him.

"Yes sir, what can I do to help you?"

The man smiled, "I am Sergeant Gomez. I am on the staff of Inspector Ramirez and I am charged with making sure you and the lovely Señora make it on to the train."

I nodded and pointed to the train station. "You may assure Inspector Ramirez that we did indeed make it safely to the train and that your mission was accomplished. Anything else I can do to help the Buenos Aires Police Department?"

Gomez coughed and looked almost apologetically at me, "Señor, Inspector Ramirez has expressed some concerns about your and the lovely *Señora's* safety. He wants me to escort you to the train personally." He held up his hands, "I know this sounds foolish, but I follow orders. I am but a humble Sergeant and it would not do for me not to follow the Inspector's orders. I am sure you understand."

By now, Morgan had decided to join us, I turned to her and said, "Sergeant Gomez wishes to accompany us to the train. There are apparently some concerns about our safety, can you believe that?"

Morgan beamed, "How delightful. Why thank you, Sergeant. How very kind of you to be so concerned about two simple tourists. Will you be joining the Señor and me on our trip to Mar Del Plata?"

Gomez shook his head, "Alas no, Señora. I am only supposed to be sure you reach the train safely. I then have to report back to Inspector Ramirez."

"What a pity," replied Morgan.

We entered the station and were exposed to a cacophony of sights and sounds. Passengers were chatting, Red Caps were hauling luggage to the various trains, and the public-address system seemed to be booming messages nonstop. There appeared to be an active police presence, but given all that had happened the past few days, it really wasn't surprising. It was nothing heavy-handed, they would stop someone for a moment and talk with them and then move on. We were not even stopped.

Once we arrived at the train, I handed the conductor our tickets. I turned to Sergeant Gomez, "Thank you for the escort. I shall tell Inspector Ramirez you did a fine job making sure we safely arrived," I smarmed.

"It was nothing, Señor. Always glad to help tourists."

Morgan held out her hand and Sergeant Gomez took it and kissed it. He smiled at Morgan, "I hope you have an enjoyable trip." He looked at me and glowered, "And you too, Señor." He tipped his hat, smiled once more at Morgan and then left us at the train.

As we boarded the train, I turned to Morgan, "You seem to have a big fan club around these parts."

She giggled, "I wouldn't have it any other way."

The train ride was uneventful and the scenery was beautiful. The train seemed very swank considering the roughly six dollars we had paid for the tickets. We grabbed a bite to eat in the club car and then returned to our seats. Morgan took out a book and I began to doze. I didn't wake until I felt the train lurch. A conductor came through the car making an announcement.

I looked at Morgan quizzically.

"He says we just entered the Mar Del Plata complex and we will be arriving at the terminal in about ten minutes."

When the train finally stopped, we joined the rest of our fellow passengers in getting off the train. We left the station and hailed a cab. We were at our hotel ten minutes later. A doorman opened the cab door for us and said, "Welcome Señor and Señora. Do you have any baggage you will require help with?"

I shook my head as I slipped him a small Argentine note, "No thank you, we are fine."

The doorman headed toward the entrance of the hotel and opened the door for us. We headed for the check-in desk. The lobby was virtually empty, which considering the hour, just short of midnight was not surprising. People were either asleep or out enjoying the nightlife. I spied a plump middle-aged woman who was standing behind the desk. Her name tag said Rosa and she was an assistant manager according to her name tag.

She smiled broadly at me, "Good morning, Señor. How may I help you?"

I laughed, "It's that obvious we are Americans?"

She maintained her smile, "No, Señor. But when I see people who I think are tourists, my experience tells me they generally will speak English." She smiled, "At least at this hotel. Do you have reservations?"

"Yes. Under the name of Rixey."

She punched something into her computer and nodded, "Ah yes. Señor and Señora Rixey. Two nights. If you would please show me some identification and sign this sheet," she said as she handed me a form to sign. I showed her my passport. She nodded and asked, "One or two keys?"

"Two will be fine."

She handed me an envelope with 463 written on the cover. "Will you be needing any assistance in getting to your room?"

I shook my head no and we headed for the elevator banks. We found an open door and I pushed the button to get us to the fourth floor. Only the elevator music broke the initial silence.

As we rode up, Morgan asked me, "Is everything okay Miller?" You didn't seem your usual self on the train ride."

"Just a lot of things happening to me on this case that never happened before. I had drawn my weapon twice in sixteen years and never had to fire it. On this case, I have killed five people?" I shrugged. The elevator arriving on the fourth floor mercifully interrupted our discussion. The door slowly slid open. The corridor was much the same as it had been in our hotel in Buenos Aires. I looked at a floor map. 463 was in the center of the floor.

Morgan took my arm and squeezed it gently as we walked down the corridor, "Listen Miller, every person you killed deserved it. If you hadn't, we both would have been dead by now. You're one of the good guys, Miller Rixey, don't ever forget that."

"Thanks for the word of encouragement. I'll do my best to keep that in mind." She was right and deep down; I knew that the men I had killed had it coming. It was still good to hear it, though.

We stood in front of the door and I took the key out its envelope and waited for Morgan to draw her weapon before I inserted it. The indicator on the handle went from red to green and I pushed the door open. I flipped a light switch on. We dropped out bags on the floor and Morgan produced her wand and checked the room. I was about to sit down when I noticed the message light was flickering on the house phone. We had just checked into the room and we already had a message?

I picked up the phone and pressed the button and listened, "Señor Rixey, this is Rosa at the front desk, I am so sorry, but I forgot to mention to you that you had two packages waiting for you. I can either bring the packages up or you may come and get them. Once again, so sorry about the oversight."

Chapter Thirty-one

"That there is a Devil, is a thing doubted by none but such as are under the influences of the Devil." Cotton Mather

"Morgan, I'm going downstairs for a few. Someone delivered two parcels for us." I heard a mumbled acknowledgment and I headed out of the room.

I was soon at the front desk. I was promptly greeted by Rosa, "So sorry, Señor. I should have remembered something for such an important guest as you."

I waved my hand in a dismissive motion, "Not a big deal. Now you said you had two parcels for me?"

"Yes, Señor. I have them right here." She handed me two packages. They were each about a foot long and about six inches wide.

"Anything else, Señor?"

I smiled, "No thanks. Thanks for remembering these."

I glanced at the packages as I picked them up. They had the same now-familiar label on them, Kaplan Cleaning Company with a Buenos Aires address. I had a pretty good idea of what was inside them.

"Will you be requiring some assistance in taking the packages to your room?" Rosa asked.

"No thanks," I can handle it, I replied with a smile.

When I got back to the room, Morgan was sitting on the couch, clad in a robe and wearing a towel around her head. She was sipping on a drink. Her eyes lit up when she saw me enter. "Miller, you shouldn't have. What did you get me?"

I chuckled, "I didn't and I don't know."

I joined her on the couch, lit a cigar, pulled a knife, and opened the first package. I had remembered seeing pictures of the weapon inside the box before but had never used one before. It was about a foot long and not very wide. There were five fully loaded magazines, a suppressor, a regular scope, and an infrared scope. I looked at Morgan, "Okay, what is it? I've never seen one of these before in person."

Morgan giggled as I handed her the weapon. "I would be amazed if you had seen or used one before. It's a Heckler & Koch MP 5K. It's the preferred weapon of antiterrorist groups around the world. It's also illegal unless you have a special permit because it has an automatic setting."

I handed her the five magazines that went with the weapon. "This must be for you."

I opened the second package and found an exact copy of the pistol I was already carrying, along with five magazines, and another shoulder holster. "This must be for me. Looks like one of my friends is expecting us to have some heavy action very soon."

Morgan nodded, "This weapon will fit nicely in my purse so I won't have any problem concealing it. You sure seem to have some fascinating friends, Miller."

I nodded and frowned. "You remember in the letter Steele wrote where he mentioned the signet ring he wore?"

"Yes. What are you thinking, Miller?"

"I'm thinking that we really don't know what Karin looks like. The way we were supposed to identify her was her recognition of the ring, right?"

"Yes. That was the idea."

"How will we know if we are giving the money to his niece or perhaps another conspirator?"

"She would identify the ring, right?"

"Naturally. A great chance she would remember a favorite special toy that was her beloved uncle's."

"My thoughts exactly. I am going to make a phone call to our friend Ms. Dinisi to see if she can find us a signet ring. It will look just like Steele's except it will have an H instead of the gothic S. Good chance if she is for real, she won't recognize it. If she is a fraud, she will claim to recognize it. Make sense?"

Morgan set her now empty glass down. "Excellent, Miller. I am very impressed. Move and countermove." She yawned, "I have a few things to do. Let me know what Ms. Dinisi says." She got up and headed for her bedroom.

I dialed up Kathy Dinisi. To my surprise, she answered on the first ring.

"Kathy, Miller here."

"Nice to hear from you, Miller. Are you free?"

"No, I have a small favor to ask. You have already been so helpful; I hate to bother you."

I heard a giggle on the other end, "Well, let's see what we can do. What do you need?"

"I need a signet ring, gold, about two ounces or so, with a golden H in a field of black. Can you get me one?"

"Sure. I can swing by a jewelry store and pick one up later today It shouldn't be a problem at all. Where are you staying and when do you need it?"

"I'm at the Sheraton and as soon as you can."

"How about noon? I've got a friend who can fly me down. Meet me at the airport? I'll hopefully be there between eleven and twelve. Depending on the problems with the ring, I might be a little late."

"I'll be there at eleven. See you then and thanks." I switched off and got up off the couch. I knocked on Morgan's door. I heard her clicking away on her laptop." Come in?"

"We are good to go. I am supposed to meet Ms. Dinisi at the airport between 11 and 1. Once we get the ring, we can go visit Karin Steele."

"Outstanding. Just give me a couple of minutes while I finish reading my emails." She turned around in her chair, her robe was slightly opened and her hair was no longer in a towel. She smiled.

"Finish up," I stammered.

Did I mention the fact that in addition to being very capable and deadly, Morgan is a very attractive woman? As a gentleman never kisses and tells, let the symbols below this sentence represent the remaining of the night.

* * * *

Chapter Thirty-two

"Before anything else, preparation is the key to success."
Alexander Gruhum Bell

Morgan was gone when I woke up the next morning. I wasn't sure what she was up to; it was probably something dramatic like eating breakfast. I knew she knew my morning plans and would be waiting for me when I got back to the room. I looked at my watch and knew I had to get to the Ástor Piazzolla International Airport as quickly as I could. I was soon in a cab and heading for the airport. I knew enough Spanish to tell the driver where I was going and that was about it. His English was almost as good as my Spanish. I left my pistols behind in the room as I was uncertain about the level of security that I would face at the airport. I was glad I had when we entered the airport. I saw heavily armed security guards walking around, occasionally stopping passengers for a moment and then move on. I also saw metal detectors at each entrance to the airport terminal. It was apparent that after The Airport Massacre, as it was now known as, the Argentines were taking their security very seriously. They did not want a repeat incident. Based on my suspicions about why the Airport Massacre occurred in the first place, I had very little doubt that there would be a repeat of it.

I saw the driver's eyes light up when I gave him a hundred-dollar bill along with a dismissive gesture indicating that it was all for him. Say what you want about America, our money still gets results overseas. The driver watched me as I took another hundred-dollar bill out of my money clip and tore it neatly in half. I gave him one half of it and put the other half in my shirt pocket. He nodded to show that he understood when I pointed to a waiting area for vehicles. We may have struggled with the language barrier, but we were speaking the international language of money. I nodded and got out of the cab and watched it park in the waiting area. I took out my passport, hoping that might speed things up and then headed for an airport terminal entrance.

I passed by a couple of security guards and was soon at the entry area. I emptied my pockets, placed the contents in a plastic bin, and stepped through the detector. It turned red as it beeped. I pointed to the metal in my suspenders and the man running the metal detector nodded. He looked at my diplomatic passport and waved me on. I collected what I had placed in the bin and headed toward customs, where I was sure I would meet Ms. Dinisi. I looked at my watch, it was just shy of eleven in the morning. I took a seat in a lounge just outside of the customs area.

Ms. Dinisi arrived about twenty minutes later. I saw her tall and willowy frame as she cleared customs and was approaching where I was sitting. She certainly looked different than the last time I saw her. She was wearing wire-rimmed sunglasses, a baseball cap, leather jacket, jeans, and running shoes, not the flight attendant uniform I had met her in.

I stood up and extended my hand, "Good to see you again, Ms. Dinisi."

She chuckled and ignoring my outstretched hand gave me a hug, "Oh Miller, after all, we have experienced together, please call me Kathy."

I smiled as I returned the hug. "Kathy, it is. I know you brought the ring that I asked for?"

She pulled out a green box from one of her jacket pockets and handed it to me. "Your request seemed a little strange, but I know you have your reasons for asking for it."

I nodded as I opened the box and examined the ring. It was just as I had requested, a heavy gold ring with an H in the center in a field of black. "Perfect, just what I wanted." I closed the box and put it in my pants pocket.

"I guessed at the size since you hadn't mentioned one. I assumed it was for Colonel Steele. I knew his height and weight, so I guessed at the ring size."

I nodded enthusiastically, "Nicely done."

Kathy glanced at her watch, "I have to be leaving. I don't suppose there is any chance you will be free anytime in the near future so we can get together?"

I shook my head, "We have a very full platter for the next few days, so sorry no."

She gave me a farewell hug and began to head back toward customs.

"One quick question, Kathy?"

She turned around, "Sure Morgan. What did you want to know?"

"Are you really a flight attendant? I mean you have a multitude of skills."

She laughed in a melodic tone, "I'm hurt you would even ask me that question. A good flight attendant has a diverse set of skills. As for some of my skills, let's just say they are hobbies of mine. I am sure you understand." She grinned evilly at me as she turned back to clear customs.

I smiled to myself as I saw her clear customs. I headed back out of the terminal and looked for my cab. There will still armed guards roaming around the terminal, but none of them even gave me a second look. A very hard rainstorm had begun while I was inside the terminal. Once I saw the cab was just where I expected it to be, in the cab waiting zone, I sprinted toward it. My driver had taken a nap and when I rapped on the glass, he woke with a start. I got into the cab and handed him the second half of the hundred-dollar bill. I managed to convey to him that I wanted to go back to the hotel and he nodded. Ten minutes later, I was getting out of the cab and climbing the steps to the hotel lobby. The doorman greeted me and I nodded as he opened the door for me. I fumbled around in my pockets and gave him a couple of small Argentine bills. My motto is to keep the locals happy as you can never tell when you will need them.

I checked the front desk for messages and or mail. Having neither, I headed toward the elevator banks, stepped in and pushed the button for my floor.

I felt my phone vibrate and I pulled it from one of my jacket pockets. I looked at it for a moment and saw it was from Bobby. I sighed and pressed the answer key, a few seconds later, once the phone was in secure mode, I heard the voice of Bobby. This may not have been the last guy I wanted to hear from right now, but he was undoubtedly in my top ten.

"Miller, this is Bobby. What have you found out about Herman? I have heard rumors he was kidnapped."

Chapter Thirty-three

"Sooner or later, everyone sits down to a banquet of consequences."
Robert Lewis Stevenson

I stepped back outside to take Bobby's call, "Relax. I'm sure Steele wasn't kidnapped, guys like him seem always to have some project on the side. They vanish for a while and then show back up when you least expect it."

"Guys like him?"

"You know freelance intel types. He could be working on our case even as we speak. He told me when we met in Buenos Aires that he was going to be in Mar Del Plata today. That's why I'm here, doing what you asked of me, which is looking for him. When I find him, I will be sure to let you know. Fair enough?"

Bobby paused, "Well, see that you do. Thanks for helping out, Miller."

I clicked off and felt my nose. Surprisingly, it had not grown one bit. I smiled and thought about what I had said. I hadn't really lied to Bobby, right? I mean all I said was that I was sure that Herr Steele hadn't been kidnapped, right?

I stepped back into the lobby and used a house phone to call our room. The phone rang a half dozen times and went to voicemail. I hung up. I then walked to the front desk, displaying my room key and passport, "Anything for 463?"

The clerk briefly glanced at both and turned and looked at the mailboxes. He nodded and wordlessly handed me a folded over piece of paper. I opened it up and read it. It was from Morgan telling me if she wasn't in our room, she would be in the hotel dining room.

I entered the dining room, saw the booth she was sitting at and sat down across from her. I ordered some bacon and eggs and coffee.

She looked up from the daily paper she had been reading and smiled, "How did things go at the airport?"

"They went well. Ms. Dinisi is very efficient." I took the box with the ring out of my pocket and showed her.

Morgan nodded appreciatively, "Very nice, indeed. After what she pulled off in the Cemetery, I would have expected nothing less." I saw her shiver as she rethought of the fate we had so narrowly avoided. She took a sip of her coffee, "After you finish your breakfast, then we should head out to Karin Steele's?"

"That's the plan. We will need to cab it, though. It's pouring out there."

"Good, we can leave from here. I took the liberty of bringing down the bonds and the real ring." She slid a folded-up newspaper toward me. "I also took the liberty of bringing down your weapon and holster."

I excused myself and went to the men's room to put on the shoulder holster and then slid my pistol in the holster. I checked myself out in front of a mirror, took a deep breath, and was ready to go.

About twenty minutes later we were heading out and on our way to Karin Steele's residence. The doorman saw us and whistled up a cab. I smiled when I saw the same cab being driven by the same dark-skinned man who had driven me to the airport. It seemed that capitalism was a live and well in Mar Del Plata. Morgan and I got into the cab and she gave him Steele's address and the taxi hurtled away.

Morgan looked at me quizzically, "What made you smile, Miller?"

"Oh, this is the same guy who drove me to the airport. Let's just say, I treated him very well on the trip there. With this weather, he probably figured out that I would need another cab ride." We stopped at the address Morgan had given. I pulled out two hundred-dollar bills. I handed the driver one of them and repeated the process of tearing the second one in half before I handed it to him. The driver nodded.

Morgan looked confused, "What was that all about?"

"This is how I paid him at the airport and got him to wait for me. He gets the other half of the bill if he is here when we leave Steele's house. Pretty basic stuff."

Morgan smiled, "Basic, indeed."

We got out of the cab. Morgan supplied the umbrella and we walked toward the front door of a charming split-level house. There was a garage that didn't seem to be attached to the house. The only noise that was being made was the rain striking the umbrella. The yard had many trees and was immaculately groomed. We pushed open the gate to the property. The gate reluctantly opened as it squeaked in protest. I saw there were lights on in the house, this was a good sign. We got on the porch and I rang the doorbell. I could hear someone inside and reached into my pocket for the ring and to make sure the TASER device on my phone was operative.

The door slowly opened and I saw an ashen and skinny young lady with jet black hair.

"Fräulein Steele?"

"Yes," she replied in perfect English, but with a German accent.

I pointed to Morgan, "We are friends of your dear uncle, Herman Steele. May we come in?" I took the ring out of my pocket that Kathy had given to me, "He said you would remember the ring?"

She glanced briefly at the ring, "I would recognize that ring anywhere. How is my dear uncle doing?"

"If you could let us in, we could discuss this out of the elements."

She opened the door wider, "Oh please do come in. I am not being a very gracious hostess." She led us to the living room area, pointed to a couch and then sat down in a chair across from us.

Chapter Thirty-four

"No good deed goes unpunished." Oscar Wilde

"You speak excellent English, Fräulein Steele. You were born in Germany?"

"Yes. I was born in a small village in what used to be East Germany. My family moved here when I was ten and we have lived here since I was ten. My schooling took place primarily in England."

I nodded, "Your parents are out, I take it?"

"Yes. Why are you here? Is Uncle Herman in some kind of trouble?"

I laughed, "Not at all. He wanted you to have this present and asked us to deliver it to you as he was much too busy to make it here today."

Morgan interjected, "When was the last time you saw Uncle Herman?"

"Well, that would have been last year. He visits me every year on my birthday," she replied with a smile.

I nodded, "Good. Well, that seems to wrap things up." I turned to Morgan, "Would you give her the envelope and then we will be on our way."

"Sure thing, Miller. I got it right here."

The woman was distracted for a moment as she saw Morgan reach inside her jacket and bring out the manila envelope. When she focused her attention back on me, I had my pistol out and was aiming it at her.

"You better hope that Karin Steele is still alive. We know you're impersonating her."

She gasped, "You are insane. I am Karin Steele. You have no reason to treat me in this manner. Now give me what my dear Uncle Herman wanted me to have and get out of my house.

I laughed cruelly, "Not a chance, sister. We are going to sit here and discuss what you did with Fräulein Steele. You gave all of the wrong answers to the questions we asked. First things first, what's your real name?"

The woman sagged in her chair, "I really am Karin Steele. I don't know why you don't believe me?"

I waved the pistol in her direction, "One more try and then we begin searching on our own."

It was at that point, I noticed she made a furtive gesture with her head toward a door that led to the rest of the house. I frowned and stood up. Keeping my weapon trained on the woman, I said to Morgan, "Keep an eye on her, I'm going to check around and see where the real Karin Steele is." I walked around the living room thinking, could I have misread the entire situation? It was beginning to look that way. I did my best to keep my attention off the door the woman had gestured toward.

Morgan gave me a strange look, "Sure thing, Miller."

"How do I get to the garage?"

The woman quivered, "It's not connected to the house. You have to go outside to access it."

I ratcheted a round in my pistol, "You better hope we find her." I fired six shots through the door and heard a male scream, the clatter of a weapon hitting the floor, and a thud.

Morgan jerked as she heard the gunshots, "What the hell was that all about, Miller?"

I pushed the door open to view my handiwork. The man's body was lying against it which offered some resistance. I knelt down and felt for a pulse. There was none. I stood up sheepishly, "Sorry about the door, Karin."

I turned to Morgan, "I'm guessing the woman we are speaking to is the real Karin Steele and this mope," I said pointing to the body, "is or was her kidnapper or something like that." I looked at Karin for confirmation.

She was still in shock but could manage to nod.

"Okay, Karin, let's do this again. When did you last see your uncle?"

"When I was three or four."

I nodded, "Your uncle said something about a ring you would remember? He said you loved to play with it when you were three."

Karin nodded, "Yes, it looks exactly like the ring you showed me, but it had a gothic S in the center, not an H like you showed me."

Morgan asked, "Why the deception?

"If you were really from Uncle Herman, you would realize all the mistakes I was making. I knew the man in the next room had a gun on me. He had beaten you over here by about fifteen minutes. I think he was expecting Uncle Herman." She shrugged, "Then you two showed up and well, I had to wing it. I couldn't very well tell you what was happening with that maniac having a gun on me."

I nodded with approval, "You are a very resourceful young lady. Luckily for all concerned, I caught that gesture you made. Well now, we have two problems. First, we have a dead body in your house and second, we need to get you to someplace safe."

Karin asked, "Why would they have done this to me?"

Morgan smiled, "Because your uncle had planned to give you this until his plans changed," she said handing Karin the envelope with 1.5 million dollars' worth of bearer bonds. "My guess is whoever was behind this wanted the money for themselves. You're a very wealthy young lady."

Karin sat in her chair speechless. Then she stammered, "Why me?"

"Because you are his favorite niece?" I suggested. "He didn't share that with us."

Morgan looked at her watch, "Now Karin, I want you to pack an overnight bag. Take anything of personal value to you. I doubt you will be coming back here for some time, if ever."

"Morgan, go up with Karin and help her pack. I need to make a phone call and see if we can dispose of the body." I shook my head; this is going to be expensive and getting to be a bad habit."

Morgan nodded and headed upstairs with Karin. I waited until I heard a bedroom door close before proceeding with the next part of my plan.

I took out my phone, turned it on, and moments later was dialing Kaplan Cleaning Company. Things must have been slow as the phone rang once and I spoke after a series of clicks and beeps, “Miller Rixey, The Bishop Agency, password is swordfish1236.”

“How may we serve you today, Mr. Rixey?”

I winced as I spoke, “I need a disposal in Mar Del Plata.”

“Wait one.” I was put on hold and was listening to some music. The music stopped about a minute later, “I am sure you understand there is a logistics problem with such an assignment. How many rooms for cleaning?”

“One.”

“Is the room secured?”

“For the time being, there may or may not be visitors later.”

“Understood. While we have a small office in Buenos Aires, we do not maintain a full-service cleaning crew down there. We do use a smaller firm for South America. They are quite efficient. Do we have your authority to contact them on your behalf?”

I breathed a sigh of relief, “Yes and send the bill to Bishop?”

“Yes. Should there be any side problems, it will be reflected in your bill. I would expect them to be at the cleaning site in about two hours. Is there any damage to the building that needs to be taken care of? The address is? I know you are a client who has used our services before, but please do not be on site when the crew arrives.”

I gave them the address, told them about the door that needed to be replaced, and they clicked off. One problem down.

I looked up and saw Morgan and Karin coming down the stairs. Karin had two suitcases and a backpack with her. I rolled my eyes at Morgan. She smiled and shrugged. I guess people have different means for pack quickly and what an overnight bag is.

“Time to go. I made contact with a cleaning service and they will be here in a couple hours’ tops. We don’t want to be here when they arrive.”

We headed out the door and Karin locked it behind her. She stopped, “With all that went on today, I nearly forgot something that could be important. Uncle Herman had sent me a letter about a month or so ago. He told me he would be stopping by to visit me near the end of the month.

If he didn't make it, the letter said, I should give the letter to someone who showed me his signet ring. I guess that's you two. She began to sob, "I know something bad has happened to him." She unlocked the door and went back inside. She was back out in thirty seconds, still sniffling, and handed me the envelope. "There is a smaller envelope inside the larger one that I didn't open."

I accepted the envelope, "Thanks. Umm, what about your parents. We cannot have them coming back and interrupting the cleaning company?"

Karin looked confused, "Cleaning company?"

I nodded, "Yeah, well we can't go around leaving dead bodies in people's houses. The cleaning company will be here to remove the body, tend to the door, and wipe up the blood. Your parents will never realize what happened here. Now, where are they?"

"They recently moved to England, which might not be a bad place for me to visit, now that you mention it."

"Do you have your passport?" Morgan asked.

Karin nodded, "It's in my backpack."

Morgan said, "Miller and I will make sure you get to the airport and can make your connections. Just call your parents and tell them you decided to join them for a while." Morgan looked at me, "What do you think, they can come back in a few weeks?"

I nodded, "Yeah. My guess is we will have this case wrapped up soon and she won't be bothered by the group that kidnapper was with again."

We took Karin to the airport, made sure she was going to be able to make it to England, watched her plane take off, and then headed out back to our cab. As we walked back through the airport terminal, Morgan said to me, "Karin and I had some time for some girl talk when we were in the restroom."

"Yes?"

"As you know, I have been working in London and have made my own fair share of contacts. She was going to have a problem depositing that much in bearer bonds in a bank. It would set off a series of anti-terrorist alerts and a bunch of other unpleasantness. I gave her the name of the bank and the name of the person I use in London. That will make a complicated procedure much easier."

I nodded, "Good. So, everything will run much more smoothly that way. Good job. I hadn't thought of that.

We headed out the terminal. The rain was pouring as hard as ever. Once we saw our cab, we sprinted to it, flung open the doors and got in. We shortly arrived at the hotel and found there was no mail for us. We took the elevator up and once in our room, I stretched out on the couch and opened Herman Steele's letter. I could not shake the feeling that he was somehow running the show from the grave.

Chapter Thirty-five

If you prick us do we not bleed? If you tickle us do we not laugh? If you poison us do we not die? And if you wrong us shall we not revenge?
William Shakespeare

I unfolded the letter, anxious to read it. I let out an audible sigh as I handed the letter to Morgan, "My German is a little weak, maybe you should read it?"

Morgan chuckled as she took the letter from me. I saw her mood change and her face darken, as she started to read the message.

"You going to share the letter with me?"

"Naturally."

She began to read, "If you are reading this letter, I have been betrayed by my employer. I am most certainly dead as my employer if nothing else is extremely efficient in dealing with what they consider problem situations. I was never mad about anything that happened to me. There was no reason to be. I always got even. I implore you to avenge me."

I shook my head, "I see our Herr Steele still likes to control events, even from the grave." Without thinking, I grabbed a cigarette and fumbled for my lighter. After a few attempts, I got the cigarette lit. "This letter was written for someone in particular and it wasn't us."

Morgan nodded, "Agreed. Maybe that explains the group of people who came to the hotel room as we were leaving." She shrugged, "His employer first searched the room and found nothing, but I have a feeling the second group knew exactly what they were looking for and where it was. I am certain that when he talks about his employer, he isn't referring to Bobby Layne."

"Makes sense to me. I doubt if his employer would be going back for a second look. Good chance their loyalties were with only Herr Steele. Probably former STASI or some such types like that. Go ahead and keep reading."

Morgan continued, "By now, you have delivered the certificates of deposit to my niece; otherwise you would not be reading this latter. I also hope you followed my instructions on getting Karin to a safe place."

"The coordinates of my now former employers base are 776, 137, 337. You will find it's about one hundred twenty kilometers from Mar Del Plata. I have been there several times, but have never been very far inside. I receive money and orders from whoever is running the show, but always through an intermediary. The opening is a cave. Be careful as while it is lightly guarded, no more than twenty to twenty-five men, there is a camera dead center on the top of the opening. To say the area is desolate is an understatement. One advantage you will have is that you will have coverage from a dense forest area that is approximately one hundred meters from the entrance. I recommend a nighttime attack."

"All I know about my employers is that they are experimenting with an artifact. Some of the men have boasted to me that it has great powers, but the men I have talked to have no idea what this artifact is. The artifact will be your reward if you are successful."

Morgan folded the letter and looked at me, "That's it." So, what do you think?"

I nodded slowly, "I need to call the concierge and arrange a suitable car rental for traveling in the country. We have some work to do before we leave on our excursion. I think we have discovered where Caesar's Medallion is."

Chapter Thirty-six

"You cannot create experience. You must undergo it." Albert Camus

As I reached for hotel room phone, Morgan reached for my hand, "I need you to explain to me how you came to the conclusion you did. I feel like I am missing something."

I nodded, "You remember the conversation we had the first night we met?"

"Our first night together would be hard to forget, any of it." She sat there, silently recalling all that I had told her the first night. She smiled and patted my hand, "Go ahead and make your call. Even if the artifact the letter talks about, isn't Caesar's Medallion, and it sure sounds like it is, it's going to worth a lot of money. Whatever it is, it seems like there are a lot of people going to a lot of trouble to keep us away from it."

"My thoughts exactly. I mean it seems like we have two groups in play, both doing their best to keep us away from the Medallion or eliminate us. We have Steele's group and the group in the cave that would just as soon see us dead. I don't think we are winning any popularity contests. Even the cops seem put out by us."

"Agreed. Go ahead and make your phone calls, I will try to locate the cave on a map. I hope Steele used standard coordinates and not some old-time STASI ones. I got work to do." Morgan stood up and started to head to her room.

"Before you go, what's the range on your H-K?"

She stopped and turned back toward me, "Around 200 yards. With a scope and if we are only 100 yards away, I cannot imagine I will have trouble hitting anything I aim at," she said with a wry smile. "I guess that once I put out the camera, they will be sending men out to investigate." She shrugged, "Too bad for the bad guys."

"That's good to know. You work on the maps and routes and I will work on getting us a vehicle. I am guessing we will want something that can handle rough terrain."

Morgan nodded and she headed back toward her room.

I picked up the room phone and punched zero, "Concierge desk please."

"Yes, Señor, right away." I heard a click and then silence as my call we being transferred.

"Concierge, may I help you, Señor?"

"Yes. This is Miller Rixey, room 463. We are planning an excursion to the countryside tomorrow and would like to lease a vehicle. We are also thinking about using it tonight too. Any idea of what type of vehicle you can get us and what time it can be available? By the way, in case it matters I can drive either a standard or an automatic transmission. In fact, if we are going to be out off the beaten paths, I would prefer a standard transmission.

"Please hold, Señor." Some unknown to me easy listening music began playing as I waited. "Thank you for holding, Señor. We found a vehicle you should be interested in. It's a Jeep Wrangler. Very reliable and it's virtually new. Would that be to your satisfaction?

"Yes. That would be fine. Does it have a navigating device in it?"

"Yes, Señor."

"Great. What time can you have it here by?"

"It's 2:30 right now. I can send an employee out to pick it up and have it ready for your use by say 5:00? Use the credit card that you have on file with the hotel?"

"Yes, that will be fine on both counts. Thank you and please call the room when it's here." I hung up. I saw Morgan come out of her room carrying a printout.

"What did you find?"

"Steele used regular coordinates. The entrance to the cave was relatively easy to find, once I knew what I was looking for. We are going to be out in the boonies, but until we hit the forest that surrounds the cave, it will be roads of sorts." She smiled, "I think we would call them paths in the States."

"Fair enough. I was able to get us a Jeep Wrangler that has a navigation system in it. We can punch in the GPS coordinates and not have to stay glued to the map. You did get the GPS coordinates, right?"

"Sure did," Morgan said waving the printout at me.

"One thing I had been thinking of was that we never did search Steele's room in Mar Del Plata. I'm not sure that what we could find there would be worth the exposure and possible risk." I shrugged, "I would hate to blow everything we have up to this point.? I mean, we have everything it would seem like right we need now, right?

Morgan nodded, "I agree. Once we got the letter he sent to his niece, I doubt that we could find anything of any value in his room."

I stretched, "I don't know about you, but I plan on taking a nap and suggest you do the same, we got a long night ahead of us."

Morgan bent over and gave me a peck on the cheek. "See you in a few hours."

I got up and headed toward my room. My phone began ringing, I sighed. I pulled it out of my pocket and saw the phone number for Bobby Layne flashing on the screen.

Chapter Thirty-seven

"It takes less courage to criticize the decisions of others than to stand by your own." Atilla the Hun

"Yes, Bobby. What do you need?" I asked trying to keep the exasperation out of my voice, after all, he was my client.

"Are you still looking for Steele? I have reason to believe he is hot on the trail of the Medallion."

"Bobby, I put the hunt for Herman on hold. I am checking out my own hot lead on the Medallion. I think I may be close."

"I don't like losing employees. You need to find Steele."

"Look, Bobby, I can abandon my pursuit of the Medallion and go looking for Herman if that's what you really want. I don't think it is. Also, we would need to renegotiate our agreement. After all, you retained the services of the Agency to find the Medallion, not to hunt down missing employees, "I replied in an even tone.

Sounding like he was somewhat brought back to his senses, Bobby replied in a calmer and more reasoned tone, "No, Miller. I need you to find the Medallion, that's your number one priority. Where are you?"

"Mar Del Plata. I'm getting ready to check out the various leads in a bit. I'll get back to you as soon as I learn something. I promise."

"See that you do," Bobby snapped.

I clicked off and sat on my bed. I had lied to my client. My general rule is always to be truthful to them, but like most rules there are exceptions. I knew there would be nothing but difficult questions about the death of Steele. Bobby didn't realize that Steele was really working against him. Telling him about the letter Morgan had found in his hotel room in Buenos Aires would only muddle the issue. As for our rescue of Karin Steele and the subsequent letter we recovered, that was something best left to Morgan, Karin, and me. Yes, I thought as I laid down to rest my eyes for a moment, deny everything, concede nothing, and keep it simple.

I heard a knock on my door. Still a little groggy for what I was sure was a short nap, I woke up and glanced at my watch. I had been asleep for almost three and a half hours. The knocking persisted, getting louder and more annoying. I said something that I was sure would not be received in polite circles and slowly got to my feet. I flung the door open and there stood Morgan, decked out in a completely black outfit.

She smiled at me, "Don't worry Miller, I have been busy while you were sleeping the evening away. I got the phone call from the concierge and our vehicle has arrived. I loaded ponchos, vests, and the rest of our supplies and made some modifications to the Jeep."

"What did you do?"

"Nothing permanent. I made sure the interior lights won't come on when the door opens and fitted the headlights with a red filter. You can still see, but it's going to be difficult for others to see us. That shouldn't be much of a problem as there is virtually no traffic in the city and once we get outside the city, there should be zero traffic on a night like this."

I nodded and looked out the window, "Good. I assume it's still raining?"

Morgan nodded and sighed, "But much like our visit to the Cemetery, the bad weather will work in our favor."

"Okay, I need to get dressed and we need to get going."

Twenty minutes later, we were heading down to the lobby. Despite being dressed in black, we didn't seem to attract any untoward attention from either the clerk or other guests in the lobby. Our Jeep was sitting in the circle drive of the hotel. I was surprised until I saw Morgan hand the doorman a wad of Argentine currency and saw him tip his cap to her.

It was going to be an ugly night that's for sure. I could hear the peal of the thunder and see the sky light up from time to time with lightning.

We got into the Jeep and I watched Morgan punch in the GPS coordinates into the navigator. She sat back up, belted herself up and we were off. The traffic was as she had predicted, very light. No sane person would be out on a night as ugly as this. Adding to the charm of the night was the fact that no stars were visible due to the heavy cloud cover. Within twenty minutes or so, we were outside the city limits. What I could make out of the city lights had soon disappeared. I looked around and seeing no other vehicles around, I pulled over.

"Hand me my pistols and the two holsters?"

"Sure thing," Morgan reached into the backseat and grabbed them along with six magazines. "I also have your vest, ski mask, eye black, and a black poncho for you later."

I put the holsters on, popped out the magazines, and nodding with satisfaction popped them back in and put the pistols in my holsters. I was already wearing a combat belt that had plenty of room for me to secure the six magazines. I looked over at Morgan, she was attaching a scope and suppressor on her H-K. She also had her pistol in a holster. Until we stopped and had to proceed on foot, we were good to go.

I started the Jeep back up and we drove saying nothing to each other. The only sound coming from the pitch-black night was the steady staccato of the raindrops on the roof of the Jeep. I was pleasantly surprised by the quality of the road we were on, sure we took some bumps and hit some potholes, but for the most part, the road was in pretty good shape. I could see the flickering of lights coming from the few houses that were scattered in the area. Other than that, there was no break in the monotony from the darkness. The thunder and lightning resumed. I would take an occasional glance at the navigation device. All things being considered, we were making good time.

We traveled for another hour or so and began noticing the beginnings of the forest that Steele had talked about in his letter. The weather seemed to sense we were close as the rain started to pour so hard, it was hard to even see down the road.

I spoke the first words either of us had said in some time, "We are about two miles south of the cave entrance. We go maybe another mile and then head into the forest on foot."

Morgan nodded and reached into the backseat and pulled up our ponchos, ski masks, and eye black. She placed them on her lap. We stopped a couple of minutes later. She removed a device from her pocket and attached it to the dashboard of the Jeep. She then handed me a device that looked like a small smartphone. She turned her device on, heard a beep and then shut it off.

"Assuming one or both of us make it out of here alive, turn that on the device I just gave you. It will allow you to home in on the Jeep. Without it, we could be wandering around until the sun came up."

"Gotcha."

We quickly put on our ponchos and ski masks applied our eye black and headed off toward the cave entrance. The weather had taken some mercy on us as the pouring rain had changed into a fine mist. It was miserable to be out in, for sure but was still a welcome break from the torrential rain that had been falling. Morgan kept a close watch on the compass and raised her hand just before we hit the clearing. We both dropped to our knees at the same time. I took out a pair of binoculars and adjusted them as I tried to make out where exactly the camera over the mouth of the cave was located. I saw a flashing red light off in the distance. I prodded Morgan to get her to look the same way I was. She nodded as she pulled out her rifle. I held my breath as I watched her take aim and then readjust her scope several times. We had finally been able to bring the battle to the enemy and we both realized we would have exactly one chance to succeed. If this attack failed, they would undoubtedly move from this location and might never be tracked down again. Whoever was inside that cave had gotten lazy over the years. I guess that's natural after so many years with nothing ever happening. I hoped it would be a fatal mistake on their part. I was able to make out two guards stepping outside the mouth of the cave. I saw flashes of light that had to be either matches or a lighter. Good move, I thought, smoking on guard duty, especially at night. Their night vision would be destroyed for a while.

I saw Morgan aiming the rifle again, she took one deep breath and squeezed off a burst. I saw the camera explode and the red light go out. Then I heard an ear-piercing siren go off.

Chapter Thirty-eight

"The greatest trick the Devil ever pulled was convincing the world he didn't exist." Charles Baudelaire

I froze when I heard the blaring of the sirens. What the hell, I thought. This was not something I had been prepared for. The question now became, what else was I not prepared for? The sirens stopped about a minute later. The message had been sent, there was an intruder about, and outside of attracting some unwanted attention, there was nothing more to be gained by having them go off. I was grateful when the sirens stopped and silence returned to the area.

I adjusted my binoculars to focus solely on the two men that were outside the cave entrance. I could see them frantically surveying the area in panic. They found and saw nothing. We were in black, they had no night vision, and the suppressor on Morgan's weapon concealed the muzzle flash.

I heard two clicks coming from Morgan's weapon. I kept my eyes on the two guards. I saw the first guard's body jerk as if he had been hit by a surge of electricity. His arm flew up releasing his weapon. A second later once his body stopped jerking, he slowly collapsed to the wet ground. I could see the look of horror on the second man's face. Well not for too long, anyway. I heard another click and watched his head disintegrate.

Five more men emerged from the cavern. Three died before they could even take a step outside the cave. The remaining two decided to rethink their strategy and headed back inside to the comparative safety of where they had come from. The cloud cover broke, bathing the area in the moonlight. That only lasted for a few seconds and soon we were back in the same situation we had been in, pitch black and the only sound we were able to hear was coming from the rain as it struck us without mercy. I had never been in a forest where I could not hear any sounds coming from the fauna that I knew had to exist here.

I finally broke the silence by removing my pistols from their holders and making sure I had a round in the chamber for each. I pulled back the slide on both weapons and now was set. I looked over at Morgan who was fumbling with her magazines as she sought to replace the one she had used on her initial attack.

"Morgan, what do you think?"

"I think if Steele was right, and he has been so far, there are no more than fifteen to twenty men left, plus whatever group they are guarding. I guess that we give the ones inside a few minutes to figure out what they are doing. We may get lucky and anyone who leaves is one less person we have to kill. I say anyone smart enough to leave, we let them leave. What do you think, Miller?"

"I agree."

After about ten minutes, we saw six men sprint out of the cave. They had no weapons visible and I guess we're counting on our mercy not to shoot them down like the dogs they were. They stopped running about fifty yards from the cave entrance and pulled off a camouflaged tarp that we had missed. It revealed a Land Rover. They quickly got in and leaving the lights off, disappeared into the forest. Their gamble had paid off and they would live to sell their services another day. I was sure we would find a road or a path had been cut through that section of the forest.

Another ten minutes passed and no other men had left. I turned to Morgan, "Stay in the forest until we find that road that those guys took to get out of here and then hit the entrance from that side?"

She nodded, "That's pretty clear cut."

We got up and began to work our way through the forest. I got smacked in the face a few times by soaked branches and the fact that the rain made the ground in the woods feel like we were walking through a bog made our progress very slow. The only noise we could hear came from a combination of the rain and the squishing sounds we made as we worked our way to the road. We finally saw the road and stepped on it. It felt good to be walking on solid ground again. We noticed a small and what looked like abandoned shack across the road. I pointed to it and Morgan nodded.

We entered the shack. It was nothing out of the ordinary. It had a table four chairs, and a bare lightbulb hanging above the table. I refrained from finding out if the lightbulb still worked. Morgan pointed to me and motioned for me to take a seat. I did, she reached into her backpack and took out a towel, some dry shoes, and some dry sox and handed them to me. That girl thought of everything. I saw her remove a set identical to the set she gave me. A few minutes later, my morale score had risen many levels and I am sure hers had done the same. We had caught another break; the rain had slowed down to only a heavy mist. Slowly, we worked our way to the cave entrance. We had caught a break, the road we had found ran all the way to the mouth of the cave. Once we were just outside the cave, I drew both my weapons and Morgan still had her H-K drawn. We heard nothing. I motioned for us to enter, we came in low and there was nothing. Once inside the cave, it was well lit, albeit with red-filtered lighting. We looked down the corridor of the cave. It looked like it ran about one hundred yards or so and then broke off into a T. We continued down the hallway until we were about five yards from the T. I held up my hand and Morgan stopped behind me. I had detected two shadows standing to the right of the T and two standing to the left of the T. I motioned for Morgan to take the ones on the left and I would take the ones on the right.

We sprang into action. I fired both pistols, aiming for the head and the two men on my side never knew what hit them. Their heads blew up and they dropped to the ground. I hear the whisper of Morgan's suppressor as she took down the two men she had been assigned. So far, so good it seemed. Now that we were at the proverbial cross in the road, did we go right or left? I opted for the right. We continued down the corridor and it looked like I had guessed right. There was a series of doors on the sides of the wall. They were opened and we looked inside. Looked like sleeping and mess facilities for the guards. No one was inside, could they be waiting for us in what looked like the main room? We would find out soon enough. I heard voices coming from the main room.

I whispered to Morgan, "When I pop this door open, come in low and come in firing. I'll do the same."

She nodded and readied herself. I turned the handle on the door and was pleasantly surprised when the room wasn't locked. I pushed the door open and dove for cover behind a desk. I pulled out my pistols and began firing. I saw Morgan out of the corner of my eye do the same. There were seven men in the room. Six of them died quickly. The seventh had ducked behind a large wooden desk. Once the firing had stopped, the seventh man arose from behind the desk. His back was facing us like he was daring us to shoot him. He held a detonator in his hand, his bony finger pressed on the button.

, "Herr Rixey and Fräulein Burke, let me warn you. If you shoot me, I will drop the detonator or lose my grasp of on the detonator. The entire complex will be destroyed. I have planned to leave this complex for another one that is more suitable for my tastes. I suppose I should thank you for killing the men who were supposed to be guarding me. I was going to have to eliminate them anyway. They knew of my new planned location."

The man turned around. He smiled, but his smile had no warmth in it. He was wearing Caesar's Medallion around his neck. "You Herr Rixey, have been nothing more than a pain in the ass and I will be so delighted when you and the Fräulein are no longer with us." The Speaker was dressed in a Nazi uniform right out of the World War II films. I blinked, I had to be seeing things. I blinked a few times, but the figure was still there. How could this even be possible? I had seen this figure literally thousands of times in various history shows.

The speaker, Adolf Hitler, cleared his throat as he waved the detonator, "Now if you will be so kind as to put your weapons on the ground, we can bring this evening to an easy and final solution."

Chapter Thirty-nine

"All that we see or seem is but a dream within a dream."
Edgar Allan Poe

I glanced around the room. It was a shrine to Hitler and Nazism. Oil paintings of Der Führer, Himmler, Bormann, and about ten other Nazis I didn't recognize. There were other memorabilia of his criminal past for all to see. Items such as small statues, framed pictures of Hitler and his various henchmen, various awards he had either given himself or been awarded, and a giant Nazi flag hung on the wall to my right. There were several desks, surrounded by chairs. The room was lit with two chandeliers. I kept my pistol trained on Hitler.

"Not a chance. I'm not leaving here without that Medallion," I snarled.

"You realize you cannot kill me. I am immortal as long as I wear the Medallion. So, you see, all of the great work you have put in this case is lost, "he sneered.

I remembered back to when Bobby had told me about how Julius Caesar had been wearing the Medallion when he had been murdered by Brutus. Obviously, the Medallion's power had not been immorality but instead had been the extension of life. I decided to keep that secret to myself.

"Herr Rixey and Fräulein Burke, you must drop your weapons immediately. I command it," he screamed. When he saw that neither of us would lower our weapons, he changed his tactics, "I have incredible wealth for the both of you. All you have to do is let me pass."

I nodded, "Perhaps you do. Why don't you tell us what happened to Eva Peron?"

"Our experiments to bring her back from the dead failed. We tried cloning but lacked the technology. We attempted to revive her. Nothing worked. Her body has long since been disposed of."

I began slowly, my weapon still aimed at Hitler, "Let me tell you something, Herr Hitler. When you attack and nearly kill a member of my Agency, it's up to the other Agency members to do something about it. If the attacker goes unpunished, it's bad for business for all private detectives. Do you understand?"

His eyes locked into mine, his jaw clenched in defiance. "Herr Rixey, you clearly do not understand the big picture. Some lives must be lost if I am going to save the world from itself. Surely, as a man of the world, you must understand that. It was nothing personal. I had to eliminate your Herr Bishop, you and the Fräulein. You threatened my movement. I had no choice but to order the death of Herr Bishop. Now I will personally have you and the and the Frau executed. My movement is more important than any single life."

"You somehow escaped justice, I can't … won't permit it again." I squeezed my trigger and sent three rounds toward Hitler, aiming for his head. All three hit the mark.

I saw what was left of his face forever frozen in a combination of shock and disbelief. His body remained upright as if the message that he was dead had not been transmitted to his body. Finally, as if in slow motion, his body began to topple to the floor. I saw his hand relax as the detonator fell from his hand. I lunged for the detonator, too late! I saw it clatter and bounce twice off the cave floor. I breathed a sigh of relief. No explosion. I moved quickly to remove the Medallion from around Hitler's neck and then quickly pocketed it.

I stood over his body, "This is for Willard." I fired three more rounds into him. Satisfied that this time; Adolf Hitler was indeed dead. I felt a sense of relief surge over me. We had what we had come for; now it was time to deal with getting out of the cave with the Medallion.

My relief was short lived. Moments later, there was a huge explosion that felt like a massive earthquake. The walls vibrated with the sounds knocking the paintings off the walls and the floor shook, almost causing me to lose my balance. A massive section of the roof of the cave landed with a crash just a few feet from me. I heard Morgan scream and turned in timc to see the part of the floor she was standing on open up and swallow her. I knew I had only seconds to respond.

I staggered toward the newly formed crevice, using my sleeve to clear my eyes of the dust and debris that was caused by the explosion. I narrowly missed being stuck being struck by another section of the caves upper dome. I glanced down into the crevice and I breathed a sigh of relief when I saw she was still alive. Morgan was hanging onto a thin ledge by her fingertips. What was waiting for her when her grip weakened was certain death from the fall.

"Give me your hand," I yelled, doing my best to be overheard over the noise in the room. I hung over the crevice and extended my hand. She reached out with one hand, using the other hand to maintain her dangerous hold on the ledge. We were a couple of inches short.

I could see Morgan's sweat-soaked face looking up at me helplessly as she strained to reach my arm. It was no good. Acting on instinct, I removed my poncho and lowered one end down to her.

She nodded and placing one hand on the poncho and then slipped for a moment when she removed her other hand from the ledge. I heard the poncho tear. Morgan swore and then hung on for dear life as I began to pull her up. As I raised her higher and higher from the ledge to safety, I saw the tear on the poncho widening. I heard a loud pop and felt a searing pain rip through my right shoulder as I pulled. I saw the crevice beginning to buckle.

"Just a little bit more. Don't die on me now, Morgan." She had gone from being a total stranger to a friend, and perhaps even more in a very few days. I could not bear the idea of losing her.

It seemed like an eternity as she slowly worked her way up the poncho. It was a double race against time. Could I get her up and to safety before the poncho tore or the crevice slammed shut? I gritted my teeth and kept focused on my assignment.

A cascade of ceiling piece fell to the floor, raising substantial dust clouds. I could no longer see. I knew Morgan was out of time and I made one more furious tug and felt her body rising. Then I heard the crevice slam shut. My eyes by now were sealed shut from the dust and other filth caused by the explosion. I laid there panting, barely able to move my arm. I cleared my vision and expecting the worst, looked over at where Morgan had to be.

Epilogue

Two weeks after my return from Argentina

Things have been crazy at the Agency since my triumphant return from Argentina. In addition to my regular cases, I am getting calls from special clients for more exotic cases. Even though I know enough to claim the mission ever happened, somehow those in the positions of power seem to know all about it. I am in a hurry to get as much done and cleared up as I can as I need to leave for Washington D.C. in a few weeks. It will be great to see Morgan again and to collect the promised reward for finding Caesar's Medallion finally. There are also some side issues that arose from the mission that needs to be resolved.

I discussed all that went on in Argentina with Willard. He agreed with Morgan and me that was a topic best left untouched. These are things that the client really needed to know. All the client needed to realize was that I had recovered the artifact he had paid me to recover. How I got to that position was not any of his concern.

My most promising case seems to be a pretty safe one. I mean, how hard can it be to find an egg? Sheesh. The client wants to hire me, but is meeting some resistance from her family. They want to exhaust all of the law enforcement resources first. I warned her that that's fine, but the clock is running on my being able to recover her item. Hopefully, she will have an answer for me by the time I come back from Washington. She kept trying to pump me for information about the Argentina adventure. The fact she even knows about an experience of mine that never happened tells me she is very well connected and informed. I just put on my best stupid face and sat there alternating between silence and denial of the trip. That's what won her over to me I am pretty sure. She knew I would keep my mouth shut. While I do enjoy a good chat, certain subjects are off-limits, such as my client's business. Not many clients will hire a detective agency that cannot keep their traps shut.

I am happy to report that Willard made a full recovery. He insisted that I continue to run the Agency and that he was going to be semi-retired, whatever the heck that means. He has been valuable in helping me keep my sanity in these crazy times. He has suggested that I need an extended vacation and that he will cover for me until I get back. I decided to take him up on that generous offer. The art objects were moved from my office to Willard's new office, which was formally my office. He left the rest of the items like the baseballs and his humidor as a "housewarming present" was I believe the term he used.

Ms. Nickels is doing well, she is driving Willard crazy as she dotes on him like a mother hen. I guess some things never change. It would be difficult to imagine running the office without her steady hand and knowledge.

Morgan and I had planned to get together before the meeting at the Smithsonian. It hasn't worked out that way. We have had time to exchange phone calls and that has been about it. She tells me she is swamped with work and also wanted to go skiing for a weekend. She invited me to come along, but my shoulder is still sore from keeping her from falling into an abyss when we reclaimed the Medallion and I am frantically trying to catch up at the office. Things are different once you assume the mantle of Boss.

Today

I stood outside the Smithsonian Institution, arms crossed and watching the traffic. Morgan had called me earlier that morning and told me she was going to take a cab to meet me. I saw a cab stop and saw her, looking very cool in her blue Army Service Uniform. I had some immediate concerns when I saw her using a cane to help her navigate the stairs. I walked down the stairs to greet her and we exchanged a brief, very professional kiss.

As she took my arm, I asked, "What's with the cane and why are you limping? Is being a Protocol Officer all that dangerous?"

"Do you know anything about skiing?"

"A little."

"Then you know they rate trails for difficulty?"

"I've heard something about it. I used to ski when I was a kid. I never got off the novice hill."

"Well, the most difficult trails are rated "Double Black Diamond. I was a pretty good skier in my time and thought nothing of trying a run down one of those trails. Well, I blew out the same ACL that I had blown out when I was playing basketball at Michigan State. I was lucky, they were able to get me into surgery the next day and here I am. I've been rehabbing it daily, but it's a slow process."

"Oh, before I forget, Willard and Ms. Nickels both send their regards."

Morgan looked a little misty-eyed. Ms. Nickels was always great toward me even when I'm sure I bugged the shit out of her. As for Willard, he's always been one of my favorite people. Well, you know how I reacted when you told me about the attack on him."

I nodded as we climbed the stairs. "What with the dress uniform? I thought your Army days were behind you?"

She looked rather sheepishly at me, "I got a call from Mr. Layne who suggested that it would be appropriate if I wore it today. He overnighted me a new one, complete with my major's insignia, and my ribbons." She tried to pirouette to display the uniform for me and nearly fell down. I caught her picked up her cane and said sternly, "No more dancing."

She looked at me for a moment, smiled, and said, "Agreed."

I pushed and held the door open for Morgan and followed in after her. We were met by an older, well-dressed man upon our entry to the Smithsonian Institution. "Mr. Rixey and Major Burke?" he asked. He consulted a clipboard that had our pictures on it. Satisfied who we were, he led us to a bank of elevators, motion us in and pressed the button for the basement.

We rode in silence until we heard a ding signifying we had arrived in the basement. We walked through a metal detector. I had decided not to bring my pistol with me and Morgan was likewise unarmed. The man frowned, "Major Burke, you will have to leave the cane outside the metal detector."

Morgan said in an angry tone, "I need it to walk, you moron. I am also Ms. Burke as I am not in the army."

I chimed in, "Aren't we being just a little silly here?"

The man spoke into a device he held in his hand. He said, "Very well, Major Burke, you have been cleared. Sorry about the cane, but I was just following procedure."

Morgan nodded, started to say something, but went quiet when I touched her shoulder.

The man knocked on the door and we heard a buzzer and a click as he pushed the door open. "Major Burke and Mr. Rixey," he announced.

Bobby looked up, "Thank you James, you may wait outside." Hearing he had been dismissed, James left. I heard the door click and lock behind me. I could taste the tension in the room and looked at the wolfish eyes of some of those seated around the table.

There were some desks in there and the walls were full of books. It was quite cold in there and I could hear the whirring of the air conditioning system at work. There were five people seated at a large conference table, Bobby, dressed in the same type of expensive suit that he had worn when we had met in my office. There was an older woman, with the nametag of Ms. Willgoose on the top of the nameplate and Curator Smithsonian Institution on the lower half. She was dressed in a while tasteful, very expensive business suit. There was a rather undistinguished looking bald and middle-aged man at the table. He wore a pink bow tie and a checkered jacket. There were two massive younger men, who did little to hide the bulges under their coats. Their suits looked expensive and well-tailored, not in Bobby class, but something I would be proud to wear. Morgan was dressed in her Army best. I was wearing my fedora, a button-down shirt, blue jeans, and my brown bomber jacket. I felt underdressed for the meeting.

Bobby pointed to two chairs, "Sit," he said. Morgan and I took out seats.

He reached into his briefcase and pulled out a passport. He slid it over to me. "If you would be so good as to give me your old passport?"

I pulled mine out of my jacket pocket and handed it to him.

Bobby looked at it for a minute and nodded. "Open yours, Miller."

I did and was very surprised to see the stamps I had gotten for entering and leaving Argentina were gone and replaced with stamps that showed I had been in England during that time. I looked quizzically at Bobby.

Bobby smiled and asked, "Is there a problem Miller?"

I shook my head no.

"Good, let's get this meeting started, shall we?"

Bobby pointed to the man wearing the checkered sports coat. "This is Under Secretary of State for Latin American Affairs, Joseph Janacek. He will explain things to you and Major Burke."

Janacek cleared his throat and began speaking in that nasally patrician accent I oh so despise. "Quite frankly, Mr. Rixey and Major Burke, if the decision had been left up to me, you would both be in prison. You two took it upon yourselves to interfere with the workings of a sovereign country, acting on your own, and without any regards for international law. You are responsible for the destruction of some pristine caves and quite frankly have made a huge mess of things. I'm sure you two committed quite a few crimes in Argentina during your stay. Luckily for you, none of this can be proved. An Inspector Ramirez seems to believe that you people were simply in the wrong place at the wrong time. I don't buy that for a second. The correct procedure in this matter was to turn your information over to the police in Argentina who had the situation well in hand and did not need your dubious assistance."

"That's a bunch of crap and you know it. Those guys couldn't catch a cold. This better not be some scam to beat me out of my fee. Everything we did was necessary to recover Caesar's Medallion, just as I had been contracted for," I shot back. I wasn't going to take any lip from some political hack.

I turned to Bobby, "You realize that had we done what the Undersecretary wanted, you still wouldn't have the Medallion."

Janacek turned purple and whined, "Bobby, do I have to take this abuse from this commoner?"

I really wanted to get out of my chair and go over and throttle this jerk, but I restrained myself.

"Joseph, you have always been a pain in my ass." Now I want you to sit there and shut the hell up for the rest of this meeting," Bobby said in a tone that clearly allowed no debate.

Bobby turned to me, "We made a deal with you and your agency, Miller and we intend to honor it fully. Now you did cause some problems when you took out that right-wing group, but that situation has been rectified. Quite simply, you were never in Argentina and Major Burke had already been sent back to her post in England. Every trace of your trip has been erased."

I frowned, "What about some of the locals who helped or knew we had been there?" I had decided he didn't need to know about Ms. Dinisi. "I mean there is that Major at the airport, our accommodating desk clerk at the hotel we stayed at, and the police we had talked to. I hope you didn't feel the need to erase them."

Bobby laughed, "They have been well compensated, there was no need to erase them as you so quaintly put it. After all, we aren't monsters, are we?

Bobby looked a little irked when I sat there, saying nothing with my arms crossed. "We have unable to locate Herr Steele. He is a most valuable asset. When was the last time you two saw him?"

I looked at Morgan and then looked back at Bobby. "I saw him last at the lounge in the bar at the hotel we were staying at in Buenos Aires." I knew that with the help of Ms. Dinisi, Herr Steele's trail had gone ice cold.

"Most strange. He seems to have dropped out of sight. Oh well, I am sure he will surface at some point."

I shrugged, "I'm sure he will turn up at some point. Those types usually do."

"Now it's time to discuss a critical issue that Joseph didn't. Word about the fact that Eva Peron's body no longer being buried in her tomb must never get out. It would cause a panic in the Argentine government and could have serious repercussions in that nation. Am I crystal clear?"

"You couldn't be any clearer. Since I have never been to Argentina, how would I have any knowledge of that?" I coolly answered. Morgan nodded in agreement.

Bobby thumbed through some papers, found what he was looking for and began to read, "The official story was about two hours ago, the Argentine Police, following a tip, were able to find the people who were responsible for the airport shooting. The group, EPFL, refused to be captured and a shootout occurred. The police sustained no casualties and the militant right-wing group members were all killed. That story is being released even as we speak." He slid a copy of the press release to Morgan and me. "This will help explain your and Major Burke's handiwork that was left behind at the site. He frowned, thirteen bodies and part of the cave destroyed? Was that really necessary?"

"Only if you wanted your precious Medallion," I glowered.

"Yes, well I suppose it was needed then. Please read this," Bobby requested. He slid a copy of the news release in front of Morgan and me.

I slowly read it, "Yes. I am sure that's what exactly happened." I turned to Morgan, what do you think?"

"I think the Argentine police did a great job tracking down the terrorists."

Bobby smiled, "Great, now since we have resolved that minor issue, let's get to why you are here today."

"The woman spoke first in a raspy voice, glaring at Janacek, "First of all, Mr. Rixey and Ms. Burke, I wish to congratulate you on a mission well done. I realize it was not very easy."

I laughed, "Ma'am, that is the understatement of the century."

She continued, "You seemed quite well prepared for this assignment. We are trying to figure out how a private investigator such as yourself could have been. I am aware of the fact that you had special intelligence from someplace. This tells me there is a security leak someplace that threatens our national security. My question is where did you get it? We had sent four other people similar to yourself and three CIA agents to look for the Medallion and none of them seemed to return. You knew something that the other people we had sent did not. What did you know and how did you find it?" she demanded.

I shrugged and sat there silently for a moment, "Look, lady, I'm a Private Investigator. It's my job to know what other people don't know. You would do well to concern yourself with your own job and not worry about my job. That's all I have to say, "I said pointedly.

One of the larger younger men began to get to his feet, but Bobby made a motion and the man sat down. "No need for that, after all we are all friends here, aren't we Morgan and Miller?" he asked.

Without waiting for an answer from us, Bobby reached into a briefcase and pulled out a sheaf of papers, and began speaking, "I hope I have made it clear that word of this mission and what you and Ms. Burke discovered must never get out. It would serve no purpose and only caus e panic and would reflect badly on the United States. We cannot have that, can we?"

Morgan spoke up, "No sir, we cannot have that."

I was still aggravated at the way the two goons had gotten to their feet so quickly, "I don't mind a reasonable amount of trouble, Layne." I paused and raised my hands, "However, at this point, talking about the mission would serve no useful purpose. I take it that Caesar's Medallion will be displayed here so that all can marvel at its beauty? I mean it is a treasure, isn't it?"

Bobby shook his head, "Not for a while. We need to study the Medallion and there are potential legal problems with the heirs of the last known legitimate buyer of the Medallion. It could be years.

"You may be selling that bullshit story, but I am not buying it. We both saw what that Medallion did," I said pointing at Morgan.

Bobby sighed, "Nothing of what you think you saw matters. Do you really think anyone is going to believe Hitler was alive in 2017? I read your report. Very well written, but it will never see the light of day. I know you were telling the truth, but it would be very embarrassing to the United States government if word of this ever got out. As for the public, you would be laughed at. People would think you were nuts and your business would be destroyed. Morgan's career would also be destroyed. Is that really what you want?"

I grimaced, "No it's not. So, what's going to happen?"

Bobby smiled again, "That's the spirit, Miller. First, Major. Burke," he fumbled through his sheaf of papers. As you were working for American intelligence, you will be awarded the Intelligence Star." He handed her the award along with a letter signed by The President. I looked at both the award and the ribbon. It was impressive. Bobby continued, "Naturally, you will never be able to wear that award in public, but I have something that will take the sting out of that. He handed her another signed letter and another small box. Morgan opened the box and saw a pair of silver eagles in it and an insignia for Colonel for her to wear on her Service Uniform.

Morgan cocked her head, as she read the letter. It was short and to the point. "Effective this date, Morgan E. Burke is 1) recalled to the Army pursuant to her discharge agreement that was signed when she resigned her commission. 2) Is immediately promoted to the rank of Colonel. 3) Will report to General O'Neil head of the Defense Intelligence Agency for staff work. 4) Order for reporting is stayed sixty days to allow Colonel Burke time to recover from injuries sustained during her last mission." Her face was flushed with excitement. She slid the letter over to me so I could read it.

"You bumped her two ranks? That's very extraordinary. I don't think I have ever heard of a promotion like that before. Nicely done, Morgan," I said with a smile.

Bobby nodded, "Well she certainly performed a remarkable job for her country. It seems right."

Bobby coughed and then smiled, "As for the sixty days leave to recover from injuries sustained on the mission, consider that a gift from a grateful country. It was the least we could do for you. Congratulations, you earned it my dear."

"Thank you. I don't know what to say," Morgan replied.

I nodded, "Congrats Morgan, or should I say, Colonel?" I asked with a chuckle.

Bobby turned his attention to me. "Now Miller, I need you to sign this confidentiality form. You will be free to discuss this case in one hundred years." He laughed as he slid my form to sign. Also, here is your wire statement for three million dollars for the successful recovery of the artifact. Per your agency's agreement with the government, it is tax-free. You should thank Mr. Bishop for making that agreement. I imagine that has saved you quite a bit of money over the years. Don't worry about the expense monies that were not spent and any other funds you may have recovered. There is no record of any of that.

I nodded as I signed and picked up the wire order. The routing numbers and my account number were correct. I folded the wire order and put it in my pocket. Bobby looked at his watch, "Now that business is concluded, I have to leave. I have another important meeting. Thank you, Madam Curator, we will be sending people over later today to collect the Medallion."

The Curator replied stiffly, "Outstanding, Mr. Layne.

Everyone stood and I knew the meeting was over. I picked up my fedora and Morgan and I left. When we got outside, I said to Morgan, "I doubt they do, but I hope they know what they are dealing with that Medallion. Its powers seem too much for people. I mean essentially eternal life? I don't like it." I shrugged as I patted my shirt pocket where the wire order was, "What are you going to do?"

Morgan batted her eyes, "I have no immediate plans. Maybe, you have a suggestion. We should enjoy what we got for completing that mission. That's how I see it. I had always wanted to get staff work at DIA, but the powers that be said I was too valuable in Afghanistan. That was why I had resigned my commission. Now for something important, I got sixty days, what are we doing first?" She laughed, "You have the money and I expect to be treated like royalty."

I pulled a cigar out my jacket pocket, clipped it and lit it. I looked thoughtfully, "Well, how about we check into the best hotel in town and order room service for a few days and then do some traveling. I got a meeting that is going to get postponed for a while. How's that sound?"

Morgan squeezed my arm and smiled, "Sounds great Miller. Just what I had in mind.

As we walked off arm in arm, I turned to her and said, "You know I never dated a Colonel before, but I guess there is a first time for everything, right?"

Morgan giggled, "Think about poor little me, I never dated a millionaire." She smiled and snuggled against me and cooed, "I'm glad to see you consider this a date."

I smiled back at her, "I hope you don't think I'm a being too presumptuous, but I arranged for your bags to be delivered from your hotel room to my hotel room by a good friend of mine. He packed very carefully and picked up a weapon for you. No one especially someone walking with a cane should go around Washington D.C. unarmed. I believe you carry a Sig Sauer P 229 Legion?"

She nodded, "I think I am going to have to keep an eye on you. You and your friends, I just don't know. You sound like you can be dangerous, Miller Rixey. Are these the friends who gave you the mission intelligence?"

"Me? Perhaps dangerous to myself, but certainly no one else, I promise. And yes, a friend provided me with those reports." I laughed.

We walked the rest of the way to the hotel in silence. We both had plenty of things to think about. Morgan had her new promotion and new duties to think about. I began thinking about the Medallion we had recovered. Was Caesar's Medallion like the Maltese Falcon, "The stuff dreams are made of," or perhaps the stuff nightmares are made of? I hoped for the former but was fully expecting the latter.

About the Author

Hugh is sixty-five years old and has been an attorney for the past fourteen years. He went back to school late in life and received his B.S. from Illinois State University in 1997, his M.S. from the same institution in 1999, and his J.D. from Southern Illinois School of Law in 2002. Hugh is an expert bridge player having achieved the rank of Diamond Life Master from the American Contract Bridge League, an avid coin collector, and loves all things noir. He has published several books dealing with the Zombie genre. This is Hugh's first foray into the Detective genre.

43980108R00103

Made in the USA
Lexington, KY
04 July 2019